Praise for *Pagan Heaven* . . .

"The first part of this literary collection is devoted to
narrative poems, which are notably contemporary, clear,
and concise. Rouff's voice is easily heard, for her style
seldom wavers; that is, each poem consists of short lines,
and is rarely more than a page long. Although her deep
feelings for those who inhabit her works are obvious, she
never sentimentalizes. Her consistency of style, paucity
of words, and culmination of each narrative, be it poetry
or prose, with a twist (not unlike that tart and tasty
lemon slice, with rind, that adds zest to a dish or drink)
are attributes that place Ruth Rouff's work on the high-
est level."

—Rosemary Cappello, Poet, Writer, and
Editor of *Philadelphia Poets*

PAGAN HEAVEN

PAGAN
HEAVEN

RUTH ROUFF
POETRY AND STORIES

GusGus Press • Bedazzled Ink Publishing
Fairfield, California

978-1-943837-44-1 paperback
978-1-943837-45-8 epub
978-1-943837-91-5 mobi

Cover Design
by

DESIGNS

GusGus Press
a division of
Bedazzled Ink Publishing Company
Fairfield, California
http://www.bedazzledink.com

In memory of my grandparents
Rouff and Fleishaker.
They embarked.

CONTENTS

POEMS

Majors · 11
Narcotic · 12
Madonna della Cucina · 14
Stonehenge · 16
Fade to Gray · 20
Aquaria · 22
Pagan Heaven · 24
Benediction · 25
Let Mike Do It · 27
Minor Ideas · 29
Mona · 30
Visionary · 32
Ball Game · 34
Ode to a Parking Garage · 36
The Bronze God · 38
Subdivision · 40
The Thirteenth Sign · 42
The Good Woman · 44
Chaos · 45
Transient · 47
Schuylkill · 49
Alma Mater · 50
Pool Party · 53
Romanov Bones · 55
Grand Tour · 57
Close · 59
On Mickle Street · 61
Jersey Girl · 63
Renaissance · 64
Penance · 66
Extremes · 67
Balancing Act · 68
Spoken Word · 71

Stories

Hermitage • 73
Replacing Phil • 78
At the Circus • 81
The Elusive Mr. Clay • 83
Spook Show • 86
Zip • 92
Great Depression • 95
When I Liked Country • 99
Romance • 105
Cute • 111
The Phillies, Dick Allen, and Me • 115
Mess with Texas • 125
Ten White Russians • 132
Immaculate • 141
Acknowledgements • 143

MAJORS

I didn't want to be a writer
in my youth. I wanted to
be a shortstop, or, at the
very least, if my arm
proved not strong
enough for short, a
second baseman, base-
woman, person?
Ranging deep
to my left, snaring the
ball on its projected
path to right, wheeling
and throwing the
runner out by a
fraction at first.
A "bang-bang"
play, as the umpires
call it, for the
slap of ball
in glove followed
rapidly by the
slap of foot
on base. A
bang-bang
play. Needless to
say, I never made it
to the Majors.

Except on paper.

NARCOTIC

It was even better than
Mister Softee, when the
mosquito fogging truck
came 'round. We
would all run
into the street
and chase it,
spinning around
in a cloud of
god-knows-what
chemicals that
left our tract house
surroundings as
momentarily
mysterious as
Foggy Bottom or
Sherlock
Holmes's London.

Few knew at the
time that we
shouldn't be
breathing that
stuff. We
took to it
like ducks
to water . . . each
child in his
or her individual
cotton candy
fantasy.

Even parents who
had an inkling
couldn't dissuade
us from the
blurring of
reality, the
softening of
contours the

clouding of

judgment.

MADONNA DELLA CUCINA

Leonardo had his
"Virgin of the Rocks,"
and I have my
Virgin of the Coke
Machine: No lie.
In Joe's Pizzeria
in Mantua, New
Jersey, a statue
of the Virgin Mary
rests atop the
Coke machine. She's
blue and white,
standard virgin
colors, and
she's standing
in a miniature
grotto. She's
not as atmospheric
or mysterious
as Leonardo's
Madonna, who
seems suffused
with an other-
worldly tranquility.
This virgin seems
suffused with, if
anything, the
aroma of
cooking grease.
But it could
be worse.

It's tough times for
virgins these days.
It's difficult to
preside over a
pizzeria.

Difficult, but not

impossible.

STONEHENGE

Though we often
used to go to
Atlantic City in
the gory days
before casino
gambling, I
can honestly
say we never
had a good
time.

It was all my
father's doing.
He got the
idea from his
South Philly
work buddies
at the Navy
Yard. They
must have
had dim
visions of
Frank Sinatra
playing the
Steel Pier
and bathing
beauties in
high heels.

But mostly
what I
remember is
a wall of
slums and
a funky
smelling
boardwalk,
presided over
by a huge
Mr. Peanut
in spats,
top hat,
monocle and
cane.

Mr. Peanut
was my friend:
walking with
my family
I felt as
bizarre
and anachron-
istic as him.
Mr. Peanut
was civil
and literate,
I was
sure.

He wouldn't
particularly
enjoy the
ocean, the
sand or
the transistor
radios that
blared Frankie
Valli and
the Four
Seasons.

Though he
might have
gotten a kick
out of my
little brother
racing out
of the Men's
Room at
the "Flaming
Angus" Restaur-
ant, my
frazzled mother
in hot
pursuit.

That was when
the toilet
overflowed
and I
puked on
the way
home.

Casino gambling
has been good
for A.C.:
the slums are
still there
but now
there's the
monoliths.

Fade to Gray

Gia and Way,
Way and Gia
two friends unto
the end, which
was sooner than
either of them
thought.

Way used to do Gia's
lips, not kiss them,
paint them, with
makeup, with lip liner.
Gia sat in a chair
while Way worked over
her, the lips, the
skin, the flawless
cheekbones. Often they'd
talk, chat, gossip about
who was doing who
Gia liked girls.
Way liked boys.
They had a lot
in common.

Gia was from
Philadelphia, the
Northeast. Way was
a gentleman from
Virginia. He was
macrobiotic he ate
miso soup it
didn't prevent him
from getting
AIDS.

Gia got AIDS, too,
from the long cruel
needle she stuck
in her arm. Religiously.
Gia, a good Catholic
girl from the
Northeast. Was a
fan of David Bowie.
Liked femmes.

There's a picture, a
photo of Way doing
Gia. Gia is
smiling, the sun
on her face. Way is
smiling too.
His long thin arm,
his meticulous hand
applying the makeup.

They look thick as
thieves.

More than married.

Aquaria

I had this idea I would
write about the
old aquarium in Camden,
not the new. The old one
had indigenous fish
that live in the slate grey
waters off New Jersey—
the kind few deigned
to see.

That is why they renovated
the place. Set aside or killed
the flounder and bass and
bluefish you might just
as soon find on
a dinner plate as
in a tank and
replaced them
with tropicals:
floating mosaics from
a Byzantine ceiling.

These are the creatures
people pay to see.
Now the turnstiles
are humming and I
find myself viewing
delicate beauties,
as well as sharks
swimming
overhead, ram-
bunctious penguins,
and one lone
alligator lying in a
tiled tank, waiting, as
we all are, for something

Good.

Pagan Heaven

Marilyn Monroe
rococo, all
pink and vanilla
floating in
the sky like
a Tiepolo
nude. Bountiful
goddess. Bares
breasts with-
out shame.
Sugary like
an ice cream
float.

I like to
believe she's
having a
pleasant after-
life. No one's
wife. A
cerulean sky
behind her.
Air is her
element. She
dwells in
pagan heaven.

BENEDICTION

I'm sitting here wondering if
I'll have to go through all
the shit my mother went through
before dying. I say
"shit" quite intentionally . . .
My mother spent so
much time on the can
it wasn't even funny.
And the money we spent
on undergarments could
have gone a long way toward
settling the national
debt.

The indignity of old
age: Ma struggling
to rise from her
wheelchair, washing
her hands at the sink,
removing her false teeth
and putting them in
a cup. Exhausted by the daily
tasks of living.

What joy was there in
Mudville at the tender age of
95?

It might be better to
crap out in one fell
swoop. Just keel
over from a heart
attack—no lingering
business.

The last time my mother
was in the hospital,
her major
accomplishment was
to kiss me before
I left for the evening.
She had to muster all
her strength to do that
one simple thing.

But I could see she
was pleased that
she did it.

That kiss was her last
will and testament.
After so much effort,

that gave her

peace.

LET MIKE DO IT

"What I need," said my
G.E.D. student Mike, "is
a little-ass book of
poetry. With rhymes."
Mike was talking with
another student. It's only
recently he's begun
talking with me. When he
first arrived in class,
he'd stare into space
as if frozen in
ice. When I'd
instruct the class, he
wouldn't react.

But now I know
his Achilles' heel:
poetry. "What does
philosophy mean?"
he asked me
Friday. He's
assembling a store-
house of words to
use in raps.

He keeps his
internal life under
wraps. Like a
true poet, he
exposes himself
slowly.

"Philosophy," I
said, "is what
you think about
life, or some other
important thing."

I don't want to
romanticize Mike.
He certainly has
his deficits, and
I've lost four
students already
this year.

Not dropped out. Dead.
My philosophy of
life is, "there's only
so much you can
do."

But I will help Mike
find his little-ass
book of poetry.

With rhymes.

Minor Ideas

In Lapland the reindeer
are mutating due to
the radiation leakage
caused by Chernobyl.
It's predicted that
in the course of
several generations
an entirely new
species will evolve . . .
lighter than air,
lively and quick,
but dwarfish,
miniature as
a minor idea.
These reindeer will
be the kind
that will fit inside
a snowflake
paperweight. When
you shake it,
the snow will fly
and the reindeer
will be
covered
entirely.

MONA

Lying in bed
on my back and
listening to my
neighbors bicker
overhead in the
most vulgar way,
I derive consolation
from the fact
that somewhere
in the North Atlantic
or South Atlantic
or East Atlantic,
fathoms deep but
not far away
there swims a
Great White
Shark—not
yet extinct and
certainly not
gentrified—
just swimming,
swimming in
cold, clean
waters—its
white belly
tissue soft but
icy, its black
eyes shifting
like ball
turrets, the
corners of
its untroubled
mouth curved

upward ever
so slightly—
a Mona
Lisa
smile.

VISIONARY

My best friend Donna
really flipped out
when served a piece
of cake with
mold in it.
This unsavory
discovery set off
a chain reaction
of voices in
her head. Telling
her she was
no good,
echoing over
and over like
banging,
clanging on
garbage can
lids.

It embarrassed me
sometimes
to have Pat
for a friend.
Those times when
her eyes, ominously
crossed at
birth, would light
up with an
unearthly
gleam.

But, all in
all, we were
co-conspirators,
like the ancient
Romans, giddily
plotting the
overthrow of
an Emperor
we would
never
see.

BALL GAME

On the round field of
Noyes Circle I hit a
pop-up which both
the pitcher and the
first basewoman
tried to catch. They
collided, smacking
together like the
closing of a book,
or the opening of
one, rather.

While the pitcher lay
prone, her beautiful
girlfriend rushed
over to comfort
her. Kneeling down
and smiling like
a Pieta, Sarah
rubbed Ellen's
exposed belly.
"Ahhh," we all
thought. "That
explains that." The
touch, so erotic
hypnotic that we
watched, circling.

Meanwhile, overhead
Anne Sexton was
circling on her broom-
stick. Sylvia Plath's
unquiet ghost
echoed library
corridors revising
everything.

There was a touch
of lunacy in the
air   a
swelling.

ODE TO A PARKING GARAGE

A wheel is a snake
with its tail in its
mouth. Just so, my
favorite all-time
parking garage is
the one at South Street
and Convention Ave,
adjacent to the
University Museum.
This is where, after
a hiatus of thirteen
years, I went
back and got my
degree via the
U. of P. It was
such fun
taking anthropology
courses there,
such fun seeing
a totem pole
after working in
a credit office.

And so, I have
a particular
fondness for that
parking garage . . .
the ramps, the
exit signs, even
the concrete booth
where the cashier
sits.

It's all impregnated
with meaning. It's
all impregnated
with effort, is what
it is.

Taking notes as
the professor talks
about how mankind
evolved. I know
how I evolved.

By getting my
ass

around.

THE BRONZE GOD

The whole thing about Roberto
Clemente is that he
was an infant when his
sister died in a
cooking fire.
Sensing his parents'
melancholy, Roberto was
propelled to "set things
right" throughout his
life. Which wasn't
long. That's why he
carried a file full of letters
from city to city.
While on the road,
he would stop
and visit needy
people in hospitals
and the like.

It's hard to
imagine a super-
jock doing that,
seems kind of
nerdy, but he
did it.

He had a private, interior
life that brooked no
opposition.

That's why he boarded
a rickety plane bound
for Nicaragua, laden
with supplies.

He wanted to make
things right.

They never discovered
his body after the
plane crashed in
the sea.

Maybe it was
pulverized on
impact. Maybe a
shark got it.

It doesn't matter.

Like a god in the
Metamorphoses, he
was transported
into air and
water.

Into life.

SUBDIVISION

Can a tract house
be haunted? I
hope so, else
what's the point
in scrutinizing
an abandoned
split-level?

Janet and
I walk across
the weedy yard,
attracted by
official document
posted in a
window. Peering
through the
cracked glass we
spy only
this: a dirty
avocado stove,
a half-empty bottle
of orange pop
lying sideways on a
table, gray
paneling and a
yellow bag of
chips.
Across the
kitchen, no
refrigerator, just
a refrigerator-
sized place. Maybe
the owners, too, were

"lost in space." Or
else some disaster,
fiscal or physical,
caused this
abrupt leaving.
And on the
warped-looking
door a gaudy
padlock to
prevent breaking
and entering.

Across the
street, a world
apart, a little
blond girl eyes
us warily as
we depart.

The sun shines
on her hair
as she stands,
clutching the
handlebars of
her bright
pink bike.
After a moment,
seeing we mean
no harm, she

almost smiles.

The Thirteenth Sign

I was born under
the sign of
Marilyn:

While she was
posing,
legs splayed
over a subway
grate in NYC,
my mother was
busy, same
week, same
year, having
me.

What would Marilyn
say to this?
I imagine
she'd look wide,
blue-eyed for a
moment, a bit
startled, then
offer up,
innocently enough
"Well, *someone*
had to
be."

Born, that is.

But I never
felt like a
Virgo . . . too
much of
a slob.

Creation is
messy, and
to the baby
involved,

birth is
an
ugly

thing.

THE GOOD WOMAN

There's no catch to this poem.
Abe Lincoln's stepmother, Sarah Bush Johnston
Lincoln *was* a good woman. You might say
she saved the boy who became the man who
saved the Union. When her wagon
pulled up to that squalid cabin in Illinois, she
saw what was needed. She strongly
encouraged Tom Lincoln to lay a wood
floor and hang a real door at the entrance,
not a dirty bearskin rug. And the boy:
Abe had fallen into sullen despair. As if
his mother's death wasn't enough, he thought his
father a dolt. Sarah became his rock. Later she
said, "Abe was the best boy I ever saw," and
that included her son.

If you go to a certain site on the Internet,
you can see an actual photo of Sarah Bush
Johnston Lincoln. She's plain as a Quaker.
There's a wary expression in her pale
eyes. Maybe she was thinking of all she
had seen. She had seen her stepson go off
to Washington in '61. She had seen his funeral
cortege return.

That's seeing.

CHAOS

California, it's like
Ovid's poem, the *Meta-
morphoses*, in the
beginning of the world
where everything, air
land and water, was
intermingled and
without form. Heat
fought against cold
day fought against
night just like
today searing fire
downs the trees and
houses, next day
floods carry them
away.

To get moralistic
you could even say
South Central L.A.
and Brentwood are
like that. Raw
passion, untouched
by reason or
restraint; mindless
flow of looting
hostile racist
cops wet their
nightsticks in
blood.

Blood flowing
sticky as syrup
on a dog's paws.

A "plaintive howl"
is heard on the
street. The dog
can't sell his story
to the tabloids and
is, thus, innocent.

Transient

A poem begins with an
image. Here's mine:
feet on a beach, someone
standing where land
meets tide. As the girl
stands, the water
sweeps and recedes, sucking
the surrounding
sand back to
the ocean until she is
left, queen of her own
tiny island: a monarchy
of one.

Anyhow, that's my vision of
Marilyn and Los Angeles:
Beauty and isolation,
a young woman
undermined by time
and tide and
by the fault lines
of strange religions,
exploitive industries,
unstable geology,
insanity. When you
think about it, every-
thing in her biography was
unsettled, soon to
come undone.

Now, decades later, in the
blooming Grove of the mid-
Wilshire district, I spy
with my little eye
a great display of
books, a coffee table
monument to
Marilyn. Will this
fascination ever
cease? (Even the
inner-city kids sport
Marilyn tees!)

I think not, for
Marilyn is the
apotheosis of
Los Angeles,
our goddess
of transience.

The Greeks had
it right. We do
need goddesses.

Not to worship or to
propitiate but simply
to represent that

which is.

SCHUYLKILL

As our lumbering bus kept pace
with the snarling traffic, we
looked out the window to
see major league beauty:

Three sculls gliding in
unison along the
Schuylkill, in a scene
out of Eakins. The
sun was shining, the
river was silver,
while on high,
the art museum
did a quite passable
impression of the
Parthenon.

"Look at those rowers," I
told the boy in the
seat behind. He craned
his neck to see. The
teacher in me wanted
him to remember this
scene all his life: a
talisman against the
inevitable ugliness.

Long after I'm
gone and the rowers
are gone and even the
boy is gone, other
rowers will row and
of course the Schuylkill will

flow on.

ALMA MATER

Before they put me out
for a colonoscopy, the
nurse advised me,
"Think of something
pleasant."

So I thought of
Vassar, me standing
on the sidewalk
facing Main Building,
a historic landmark and
heartbeat of the campus.

It is a privileged
environment. One
has to jump through
hoops just to
pass through
Taylor Gate.

And I've always loved
the alumnae. Strong-
willed women with
liberal leanings
inventing COBOL,
studying the rotation of
galaxies, inhabiting roles,
and best of all,
writing poetry.

Punctuating Noyes Circle
these days are marble
benches inscribed
with lines by
Elizabeth Bishop.
When I slow down
long enough to look,
I can run my
hand over the
chiseled words:

"If you tasted it, it
would first taste bitter,
then briny, then surely
burn your tongue. It is
like what we imagine
knowledge to be:
dark, salt, clear, moving,
utterly free . . ." *

These are the lines I
think about when
I hear of some eight-year-
old girl forced to marry.
These are lines I
think of when I hear
about "honor" killings.

Yoko Ono got that
right. Women *are* the
niggers of the world.
Utterly un-free.

So when I think of
something pretty, I think
of Vassar. An imperfect
institution founded
by a brewer.

And always brewing.

From "At the Fishhouses" by Elizabeth Bishop

POOL PARTY

It was great the time
the McIver's swimming
pool burst. It was like
an atom bomb going off
in someone's back yard
yet no one was injured.
Pool Party: The hot
young suburban couple
and their laughing
friends all crowded
into this big white
elephant of a blue
above-ground plastic
pool with their three
young sons: Manny,
Moe and Jack some-
where in the back-
ground. We were
eating dinner, I
think, when we heard
the explosion my
mother jumped, thinking
"gas" and "fire" but
instead of smoke
only water poured
forth from the McIver's
yard gushing between
the fence slats like
Noah's flood. I had
never seen so much
water short of a
river or ocean. There
was something delight-
ful about the way it

overwhelmed the
grass. I don't even think
the McIvers were mad
about it. Their defective
status symbol had done
what few other material
objects could:

it roared.

Romanov Bones

Can you imagine being
bones? I can. Just
lying, all broken
and hacked amidst the
muck. Clay seals
you in—sardines in
a tin—all comfy
cozy for seventy
years. There's really
no hurry. When you're
dead, you're dead.
You can wait
for the earth to
turn. You are
earth, almost
then they finally
dig you out.

You explode into
headlines like
dancing skeletons.
All flash and
drama. All
mystery and
romance.
"Romantic
Romanovs" . . .
deadly to Lenin.

"Stupid girls," he
must have
thought.

Well, he thought
too much
And imagined
too little.

GRAND TOUR

The Hoyt Corporation
build a huge multiplex
near here, that
went out of
business soon after
it opened.

I'd like to tour
it: wander down
the main concourse
and pop my
head in each
single theater
and stare at
where each screen
would have been,
should have been.

I'd like to observe
the spaces for the
audience, too, those
popcorn munching
multitudes, those
laughing, sobbing
hordes who now
get their fair
share of entertainment
elsewhere.

There's a ghostly
silence in
Hoyt's Multiplex
now. Maybe a
few mice, a
few rats, some
bugs.

Nothing, really,
to disturb the
eerie dream-
world without
lights, camera,

action.

CLOSE

I asked a friend to
meet me at a diner.
She said, "Is that
the body diner?' She
thrilled to think it
was the one the
mafia corpse was
discovered at.

"No." I felt bad
telling her no.
It wasn't the body
diner, it was only
the one on the White
Horse Pike. The
body diner was
off at the circle
end of 130, near
the Delaware River
and so-o-o con-
venient to Phila-
delphia.

Today I passed
the real, the
genuine body diner.

I thrilled to think
a corpse, open-
mouthed, had been
discovered there.

I speculated about
the state of the
world and the
Mafia wars. I
felt proud to
live so

close.

ON MICKLE STREET

I met a man
who knew a
woman, an old
woman, who,
as a little child,
knew Walt
Whitman in
Camden.

Wonder what
that was like?
Sitting on the
stoop with
Walt Whitman.
Having some
vague, childish
notion that
this gray-maned
old man was
different, special,
one for the
ages.

Perhaps you
showed him
your favorite
marble or
demonstrated
your knowledge
of a top?
Maybe you
came to
him with
a dirty face or
mud-pie hands?

It gets humid
in Camden. The
river gives off
a pungent river
smell. Various
merchants hawk
their wares
up and down
Mickle Street.
Fishmongers, milk-
men, bread-
men, and he
man who
delivers ice.

Walt Whitman
never seems to
do much of
anything except
sit and look
and listen.

That's why
you like him . . .
he *does*

listen.

JERSEY GIRL
(in memory of P.M.)

Our friendship was
like the night I
had to work late
at the Kmart
and walking
out to my
car, I looked
down and spotted
an elegant
serpentine
necklace:
gold and
entirely
unexpected.

Now you have
slipped your
mortal coil,
removed your
physicality like
a bracelet or
necklace or
ring.

But driving
down the street
to the convenience
store, I
think of
what a Jersey
girl you were
and, in my
mind's eye,
will always

be.

Renaissance

The best room I
never lived in
was the one
in Florence that
was lined
with Botticellis.
It was like
being inside
some sweet
genius's
brain.
Beautiful
women who
weren't
cow-like but
refined. Soft
pinks and
blues and
that coolly
resigned
tilt of the
head as if to
say, "I
deign to be
born."

Don't ya just
love it?
Wouldn't ya
like to stay there
forever? They
nearly had
to
kick me

out of

the place.

PENANCE

Peg Albertine
has been dead
a long time. She
was the leathery
faced, gray
haired dyke
who worked in
the customer service
department at
W.B. Saunders
Publishing Company
and who scandalized
all the girls/women/
chicks on the
seventh floor
with her
demonstration
of the menstrual
sponge.

Everybody thought:
"This homely
old dyke must
be out of her
cotton-picking
mind, with all
these women's
lib ideas
of hers."

If she had
been young and
beautiful and
said exactly
the same
thing, she
would have
been loved.

You know,
it's shitty
the way they
shunned
that poor
woman. She
had no
friends at all
there, in
customer service,
on the
seventh floor.

But she was
homely and
I feared her
like a
disease.

EXTREMES

I read a biography that said
that the father of the
famed photographer of
sadomasochist scenes,
Robert Mapplethorpe,
used to inspect toasters for a living.
No wonder his son felt so
compelled to
go to

extremes.

BALANCING ACT

Remember Ed
Sullivan, when he
used to have
on those jugglers,
only they didn't
really juggle
they just
balanced spinning
plates on sticks
with one
leg raised,
spinning a
hoop and
keeping hoops
spinning, too,
about their
forearms
while way up
high,
balanced on
the plates
beneath the
spotlight was
a lone,
jittery coffee
cup? And
how the
performer
would sweat
as he,
like Atlas,
balanced all
this crap?

For some strange
reason this
activity has
fallen out
of fashion.
That's a shame.
Maybe some day
I'll take
it

up.

SPOKEN WORD

I'm worried about the
land filling up. I'm
wondering where all
the dryer lint goes.
It's all the same:
shit in, shit out.
So much matter
is what's the
matter.

Exploit, expend.
Do it again.
Even computers, those
brainchildren of misfit
mathematicians, get
tossed in the trash,
sooner or later. Certain
of their elements
leach into the
soil and only
make things
worse.

Or maybe it's
just me I'm
worried about.
Me, the victim
of my own
mortality.

The only thing
that makes things
better is knowing
great poetry has
been written of
dust to dust.

From the fall of
Troy to the
Battle of Stalin-
grad. From
Sappho to
Frost.

You don't see
landfills filling
up with
alliteration or
metaphor.

Yes, we is

pretty.

HERMITAGE

I was sitting with my niece Melanie in the living room of her home in Nashville. We were talking about visiting President Andrew Jackson's house, The Hermitage. In front of us, Melanie's six-year-old daughter Sarah sat playing with a doll that was nearly as big as she was. The doll had pink skin, blue eyes, and blond hair made out of some coarse synthetic fiber. Sarah had brown skin, brown eyes, and springy soft black hair. Strangely enough, her African American grandmother had sent her the Caucasian doll. Melanie said that she had found it on sale somewhere. Hard for doting grandmothers to resist a sale.

"I don't think Sarah is ready for *that* conversation," Melanie was telling me. She was referring to the fact that The Hermitage had been a slave-worked plantation. If Melanie and Sarah went with my brother Bob and me to the Hermitage, Sarah would inevitably raise certain questions. Sarah was a bright child, alert to nuances and evasions. She was also very sensitive.

"I understand," I told Melanie. I was disappointed that she and Sarah wouldn't be joining us, but I could understand why. However, I was determined to enjoy myself. This was my first trip to Nashville. I wanted to see all the sights . . . politically dicey or no. I had been happy when Melanie and her musician husband Ken had decided to move there from Los Angeles a year earlier. Nashville is much closer to New Jersey than is Los Angeles, and I had always been curious about the "flavor" of Southern life.

The next morning Bob and I set out in our rental Pontiac, heading onto 155 East. One of the things I like best about Bob is that he never criticizes my driving. He's developmentally disabled—but he can read and loves to do so. He also loves to see sightsee. I thought he'd get a kick out of a trip to Nashville—that's why I took him along. After a few minutes on Old Hickory Boulevard, we made a right onto Rachel's Lane, so named after Andrew Jackson's beloved wife.

You can't see The Hermitage mansion from the road. You first enter the one-story visitor's center. Inside, we picked up our audio headphones and began looking around. As we did, any thought that Melanie could have avoided telling Sarah about slavery during a visit was quickly dispelled. Interspersed between exhibits of Jackson's personal belongings were placards telling about the various house slaves who had catered to him and his family. One showed Hannah Jackson, a thin, unsmiling woman who was head of the house servants. Hannah was wearing a white apron over homespun and held a walking stick in her right hand. The bottom section of her face was sunken in, as if she had no teeth. Another photograph was of Betty, the family cook, and her great-grandchildren, circa 1867. She looked grim-faced, clad in a coarse jacket and dress; the children were ragged and unsmiling.

We then left the visitors' center and walked up a path to the white-brick mansion, which was nested between tall trees. From a cheerful lady docent dressed in period costume, we learned that the original mansion had burned in 1834 and been rebuilt in Greek Revival style. It had Doric columns and a white picket balcony. Inside the large center hall, French neo-classical wallpaper depicted a scene from the *Odyssey*: the visit of Telemachus to the island of Calypso in search of his father. I had already known that the Southern aristocracy fancied itself heir to the ancient Greeks. Here was more proof.

Up the elegant, elliptical stairway, there were several bedrooms. Inside each one was a canopied four poster bed, so high you needed steps to climb into it. Adjacent to the bedroom Andrew Jackson died in was his library, containing over six hundred volumes. The docent told us that the Ladies' Hermitage Association had had to buy back most of the original furniture after Andrew Jackson's adopted son sold it to pay off his debts. Evidently Andrew Jr. had let the family fortune slide through his hands. So much for inherited wealth.

At the foot of the back stairs was a huge dining room with Venetian blinds, elaborate place settings, and a wall-to-wall cloth floor covering, the height of fashion circa 1836. Out the back door, the kitchen stood in its own small building. We were told that it had been separated from the rest of the mansion to prevent fires and to keep odors and heat from entering the house.

Outside another docent pointed out a bell on a pillar that was used to call the slaves. The docent told us that there were wires connecting rooms in the mansion to other, various-sized bells. Depending on the tone of the bell, a slave could tell in which room his or her services were requested. Then the slave would have to drop whatever he or she was doing and go to attend that person.

"What if the person was a pain in the ass?" I wondered.

Bob was content to take pictures.

Next we walked around the side of the mansion to the Jacksons' tomb. It stood within a lovely English garden. It was a Greek Revival cupola made of Tennessee limestone and coated with copper. It stood over two stone slabs . . . Andrew's and Rachel's. A few paces to the right sat another grave. This grave belonged to Betty's son, Alfred. After a lifetime spent at The Hermitage, Alfred had requested (demanded?) to be buried within spitting distance of his dead master. Since Alfred chose to stay on the property even after emancipation, the powers that be acceded to his request. It couldn't have been that Alfred particularly enjoyed servitude. Our audio tour noted that when Alfred heard a white visitor say that slavery wasn't so bad, he asked the man, "Would *you* like to be a slave?"

I speculated about Alfred. Perhaps he had asked to be buried close to Jackson because he knew that millions of people would visit the place. Perhaps he wanted those visitors to know that slaves had built it. However, we'll never know for sure, since the slaves at the Hermitage, as elsewhere, were prevented from learning to write.

Bob and I then walked over to a slave cabin. It had a plank floor, a window, and a fireplace. There was no French wallpaper depicting Telemachus's journey. There were no oil paintings or canopied bed. We had the option of taking a walk to see more of the cabins, but since the temperature was over one hundred degrees, we decided to go to lunch instead. I doubted if the other cabins would have differed much from this one. Uniformity was kind of the point of slave habitations.

As Bob and I sat eating our lunch in the cafeteria, I realized that there was no way that Melanie could have taken Sarah to see The Hermitage. This was sad, because in one respect, Andrew Jackson was a great man. He had expanded American democracy to include the average man . . . average white man, that is. But he kicked the Cherokee Indians out of Tennessee and lived in luxury while blacks lived in abject servitude. He thought that was the natural order of things. I could imagine little Sarah asking, "Mommy, what's a slave? Why were only black people slaves? Why did they have to live in little houses while the white people lived in big houses? Why? Why? Why? Why? Why?"

When Bob and I returned to my niece's house, I told Melanie that she had made the right decision.

"There's no way," I said, "you could have avoided the subject." A little while later, Melanie's husband Ken walked upstairs to get a soda. He had a studio downstairs where he produced music. Ken's family had been landowners who had been run out of Mississippi decades earlier by the Ku Klux Klan and who had eventually made their way to California. Although I didn't ask Ken, something told me that he was in no hurry to visit The Hermitage. I wondered too about him bringing his family to Tennessee. But Nashville is more liberal than other parts of the South.

"Nashville went for Obama," Melanie told me.

"People have been very welcoming," Ken had said earlier.

On the couch, Bob sat looking at his Hermitage postcards. Meanwhile, Sarah played with her white doll. She liked to lug the doll around the house with her. The doll had a stilted grin on her face. I didn't think she was a particularly attractive doll. She reminded me of a cheerleader.

"Sarah's alter ego," I said to Melanie while we were standing in the kitchen.

"Sarah likes white dolls better than she likes black dolls," Melanie admitted. "I wasn't counting on that."

I told her I knew several women, one white, one black, whose biracial children were now fairly well-adjusted adults.

"It's a process," I said.

Replacing Phil

It was difficult, when considering Phil, to know whether to ascribe his general incompetence to old age or what. It was said that he had, until quite recently, been a foreman in construction, drywall, to be exact. And now here he was, just a few months later, in retail. In the sporting goods department of a large chain store. Kmart, to be exact.

Well, he was in his seventies, that much was known. And he was a pleasant enough guy, who liked to whistle while he worked, as well as a dapper dresser, with his button down shirts and snazzy suspenders. But he was old, of that there could be no doubt. His head had that shrunken, skeletal look to it, with the remaining fine white hair clinging to it like wistful tendrils of vine.

He couldn't hear too well. If you repeated his name loudly while he was engaged in some activity, he would look up in alarm, his mouth working fitfully, and he would cry, "Well?" Not "what" but "well ." I always wondered why he would say "well" when he meant "what ." But I never asked him, for it would have been rude to. He was at least thirty years older than me. He was at least twenty-five years older than his wife, Joan, for that matter, who was a part-time checkout supervisor. Everyone wondered why she had married an old geezer like Phil, but no one asked her, of course. It would have been rude to.

We all realized that the transition from construction to retail would be hard for Phil, but we couldn't have imagined just how hard. It took him forever just to learn how to use the phone! He couldn't seem to get the hang of answering price checks. When there'd be a price check for sporting goods at the front registers, it took him forever to respond to it. At first he just didn't pay any attention to the page, and then when we had impressed upon him that he had to, it took him a long time before he could master the system of picking up the phone and pressing the intercom button and then number 17 for checkouts. Sometimes he'd press "page" by mistake and you'd hear his nervous, tentative voice over the store loudspeaker saying something inane like "Uh, Dave, how do you work this darn thing?" all over the store.

Well, I had to admit it was kind of funny when he did this. It broke up the monotony. But when he messed up on the sporting goods register, the customers tended to get irked. He was completely thrown by the registers. He would totally forget what had just been shown him about ringing up credit card purchases or checks. Even when he went back to the front registers for remedial training, it still didn't make too much of a difference. He'd still mess up big time.

Mark, a short Filipino guy who had worked in the store about three months and already knew everything, quoted a wise old Filipino proverb when referring to Phil.

"You can't teach an old dog new tricks," Mark said.

Phil became an object of wonder and amazement. One day, after he had been working in the store nearly two months, he asked the store manager where the pet department was. She was aghast, as pets was directly across from sporting goods. It was kind of amazing that anybody could be that dense not to notice it.

"I'd never have drywall done by that guy," Ted, another of my sporting goods associates, a mere kid of fifty-eight, muttered, shaking his head. We thought that maybe it wasn't just because Phil was old that he didn't pick up on things. Maybe, we suspected, it was because he was old and dumb. In fact, maybe he had been dumb all his life. Or a fourth possibility—maybe he just didn't care.

But he seemed conscientious enough. When you asked him to fill the motor oil aisle, he'd fill it. He'd put all the different grades of oil in the wrong places, but he'd fill it. And the bowling shoes. He'd fill that section up, too. Sure he'd put the $39.97 shoes in the spot labeled for $25.97 shoes, but at least he'd fill it.

"You'll go to heaven, Ruth," the store manager, Ms. Taylor, said to me one day. She meant because I had patience with boobs.

"Thanks," I said.

A decision was made to move Phil to footwear, part-time. In footwear he was assigned the task of removing tissue paper from the incoming shipments of shoes.

"A tissue paper technician," somebody quipped. But Phil was extremely slow at this task. It took him overtime hours to complete the job.

"Speedo Phil," Robbie, another Kmart associate, who was eighteen years old, called him.

"Is he really that slow or is he just milking the job?" somebody else wanted to know.

One day they had Phil filling in back in my department. Evidently a customer asked him where light bulbs were in the store and he didn't know. So he asked the assistant manager, Paul, who told me. "I'm not making this up!" Paul said. Light bulbs were right over in the home center department, adjacent to sporting goods on the left hand side.

"Something's got to be done, something's got to be done," muttered Paul. "It's a shame."

But who wants to be the one to fire someone who's old enough to be your grandfather? I mean, how humiliating for Phil, not to be able to make it at Kmart. It's not like working for a hot-shot company like Microsoft or Lockheed Martin, for god's sake, where you actually need to know something.

So right now, as I write this, Phil is still working for Kmart. Still screwing up big time.

"He's awful!" I told the store manager a little while ago.

I had never referred to any employee in that way before. We sort of laughed together in agreement. We sure hoped we didn't get as dense as Phil when we got old. We kind of thought we wouldn't.

At the Circus

I can't say my parents fought a lot, but one fight they had was memorable. It happened like this: late one Saturday morning my father stuck his head in my bedroom and noticed that my dresser top was an absolute mess. Loose change, baseball cards, crayons, and dust covered the surface like algae covers a stagnant pond. I was lying on my bed reading a *Spiderman* comic book, oblivious to everything but the adventures of Peter Parker. I was a tomboy. My father must have barked at me to clean up the mess, but I really don't remember. What I do remember is that a few minutes later, he informed my mother that she was a bad housekeeper. I guess that, looking around the house, he realized that my dresser top was simply a microcosm of the general disarray. At any rate, my mother went ballistic. She started screaming and crying hysterically. I guess you could say the old man had touched a nerve. My mother was very intelligent, had even skipped a grade in Catholic school, but had never done anything with her intelligence. Being a housewife and the mother of seven must have been very unfulfilling for her, but she could never find it within herself to do anything else. So telling her she was a bad housekeeper was like treating a wound with boric acid.

I hated to hear her scream and cry. My father decided the best thing to do was to hightail it out of there. So he took me to a circus that just happened to be performing in the nearby town of Pitman. It was called the Hoxie Brothers Circus. It was a Diane Arbus-type event. I thought the whole setup was kind of bizarre, especially the clowns, but for some reason my old man liked circuses. I guess they harkened back to his boyhood. This was when there were still a lot of circuses traveling around the country, putting on shows in canvas tents. This was before Ringling

Brothers pretty much became the only game in town—and circuses got corporate, just like everything else.

At any rate, there were clowns and sawdust and trapeze artists at this circus, and little dogs jumping through colored hoops. There must have been some lions and elephants because Hoxie Brothers was famous for them, but I honestly can't remember. Most memorable to me: there was some circus lady there wearing fishnet stockings and high heels and a tight black jacket over little black shorts that barely covered her ass. She wore lots of makeup and had curly blond hair of a brassy sort. I don't know what her official "job" was, but I remember her standing just outside the circus ring, talking and joking with people. I couldn't get over her. She was sexy and cracked wise in a brazen, pulp fiction sort of way. She fascinated me. She was so different from my mother, who wasn't sexy at all.

By the time the circus was over and we got home, my mother had calmed down considerably. I don't know if my father apologized to her or what. If they kissed and made up, I never saw them do it. Things just somehow went back to normal.

Going to bed that night, I thought of the circus woman in the skimpy outfit. I couldn't get over her. I compared her existence to that of my mother. I imagined that she spent her life smiling, making wisecracks, and traveling from town to town. How in the world, I wondered, did she get away with it?

THE ELUSIVE MR. CLAY

Unlike most modern doctors, Dr. Waslik, our family practitioner for over forty years, doesn't have a receptionist. That is mostly because he doesn't schedule appointments. Like the lunchmeat counter at Acme, it is strictly first come, first served at Dr. Waslik's. Walking the few yards from his tidy examining room to his waiting room, he gruffly ushers patients in and out. Both examining room and waiting room are located in the south section of his house, a large colonial on Delaware Avenue in Woodbury, New Jersey. Dr. Waslik, it seems, is not a believer in high overhead. He did, however, until very recently have a male secretary who did his paperwork and answered the phone. That was the mysterious Mr. Clay, whom no patient had seen for the past forty years. Small wonder that Mr. Clay incited speculation about his very existence. He was a disembodied voice, an enigma, yet a gatekeeper and therefore to be respected.

I was sitting in Dr. Waslik's waiting room one evening with a chronic cough when I learned I wasn't the only one to find the thought of Mr. Clay intriguing. A man a few years younger than myself was sitting on Dr. Waslik's old green vinyl couch with his young son. His son was fidgeting on the couch, rolling about in a frisky way, when the man fondly announced that as a child he had played on the same couch. People nodded. We agreed that, all told, the waiting room hadn't change much in forty years. The same green walls, the same cracked and yellowed linoleum tile, the same green and liver-colored armchairs (one mended now with green vinyl tape), the same magazines on the table—*Sports Illustrated*, *National Review*, *Reader's Digest*, *Highlights for Children*—a greenish-hued beach scene, and a framed replica of the letter Lincoln wrote to a young girl after she advised him to grow whiskers (Dr.

Waslik was a big Lincoln fan). I forget who brought up the subject of Mr. Clay, but the man confessed that he had never seen Mr. Clay. Nor had I. Nor had, it turned out, any of the other patients in the waiting room. We all kind of chuckled at this. We only knew he existed because it was he who answered the phone when we called Dr. Waslik's office to get prescriptions refilled or to see what time Dr. Waslik had hours that day. We all wondered where, exactly, Dr. Waslik *kept* Mr. Clay. I mean, we had never seen a suitable alcove which could have kept a secretary's desk. Of course, what went on in the house outside of the waiting room and the examining room was none of our business. Nonetheless, I had images of Mr. Clay tucked away in a closet somewhere, a musty, narrow-shouldered man surrounded by medical records, forced to labor under trying circumstances, like Scrooge's Bob Cratchit.

Actually, Mr. Clay had a voice that sounded a lot like Dr. Waslik's. Sometimes when I'd call the office, I would think it was Dr. Waslik answering the phone when it was Mr. Clay. Which led me to further speculation. Perhaps there *was no* Mr. Clay. Perhaps Dr. Waslik merely *pretended* that there was a Mr. Clay in order to impress his patients. Perhaps, Dr. Waslik and Mr. Clay were one and the same man, like a less malign version of Dr. Jekyll and Mr. Hyde. Or Norman Bates and his mother. On the other hand, Mr. Clay had a kindly voice. Dry and elderly, but definitely kindly.

I remember when I called Dr. Waslik's office one Saturday morning and Mr. Clay answered.

"My mother got bit by her cat," I said. "How long will Dr. Waslik be in the office?"

"Just a minute," Mr. Clay said. Then I heard him throw over his shoulder, "Mrs. Rouff got bit by a cat!" I could imagine Dr. Waslik halting on his way out the door, golf bag slung over his shoulder. Curses! Foiled by a nasty feline.

Mr. Clay returned. "Can you get here by ten-thirty?" he asked.

"Okay."

Well, I got my mother to Dr. Waslik that morning by ten-thirty and the cat bite was duly attended to. Fortunately, it didn't get infected. But I never saw Mr. Clay in the office on that day, or on any other day, for that matter. The last time I went to Dr. Waslik, he told me that Mr. Clay had fallen and broken his hip. Not too long after that, I learned from another patient that Mr. Clay, being elderly, had passed away.

I imagine some people must have actually been close to Mr. Clay, like Dr. Waslik, for instance, and perhaps his wife. It was strange, though. I can't pretend to know what it means. But in a subtle way I miss Mr. Clay. It's not every day you fail to meet a man like him.

Spook Show

"Tommy!" Mrs. Del Vecchio shouted at her son from the side door of their house.

"Whaty?" Tommy shouted back. He and I were playing catch with a rubber ball in the street in front of my house, which was two doors up from the Del Vecchio residence.

The "whaty" was one of the things I liked about Tommy: his cheeky sense of word play. It was a simple thing, and hardly the height of wit. Yet none of the other kids on the street—the Joeys and Bobbys and Johnnys and Debbies—said "whaty" when their mom or dad called them.

I was "Ruthie" some of the time. But my mother called me Ruth Anne, so I couldn't very well say *whaty* when she called me.

"Dinner's ready!" Tommy's mother shouted.

"Okay!" Tommy tossed the ball to me. "Gotta go."

"See you tomorrow."

I watched as Tommy trotted off toward his house. He was a nice kid, but lately I felt bad for him because of his dad. Sometimes we kids—my younger brother Sam and Joanne Muhlbacher from across the street and others—would play board games like *Sorry!* and *Parcheesi* and *The Game of Life* on the round patio table to the side of Tommy's house. As we rolled the dice or spun the wheel under the patio umbrella that shielded us from the sun, we concentrated on the rewards and pitfalls of the games. But sometimes we'd notice Mr. Del Vecchio entering or leaving his house—a gloomy figure even in the brightest sunlight.

Although Tommy's mom was always cheerful, and would sometimes serve us root beer or Coke in real glasses, I don't recall Mr. Del Vecchio ever speaking to us kids. Even though he couldn't have been much more than forty, he was rail thin, and his head was completely bald—like a cue ball. What's more, there were marks along one side of his head that I much later realized were suture marks. He never looked happy.

When I asked my mother why Mr. Del Vecchio's head was completely bald, she told me that he had a cancerous brain tumor.

"When you get radiation treatments, your hair falls out," she explained.

I guessed that was why Mr. Del Vecchio looked grouchy all the time. He had something awful growing in his head—like mold, only worse. I wondered how he acted toward Tommy. I suspected that Tommy had to be on his "best behavior" at all times, but somehow I couldn't imagine Tommy managing that. Around us, he was a lively boy.

"Ah, poop!" Tommy would raise his hands to his head and wince if his token landed on a bad square during one of our board game afternoons. Sometimes he would win and sometimes he would lose, but he was never a sore loser.

That August Tommy and I decided to create a spook show in my family's garage. Our immediate impetus was that the Kaminski kids over on Lansing Drive had had one in their garage, which we had both checked out. All they had were some threadbare sheets hanging from the rafters and some kid running around in a sheet.

"That wasn't scary," Tommy concluded. I agreed.

"Why don't we put up our own? We can use my garage," I said.

"Neat!" Tommy replied. "Let's do it!"

Another thing I liked about Tommy was that he was willing to hang out with me, a girl. It helped that I was a bona-fide tomboy and not a girly-girl who was content to play with dolls. (Actually, I did play Barbie dolls with my friend Kathy, but that's another story.)

Before we began, I asked my mother for permission. I knew she would give it. She had had seven children. I was the sixth. Micromanaging us was beyond her energy level at this point.

"Well, all right," she said. "But don't get *into* anything."

The next morning we opened the door of my family's garage and began setting up the show. Sam joined us. We had to keep the garage door nearly closed because we didn't want anyone seeing our preparations. Our "centerpiece" was a dark blue, battered trunk I had taken to camp a few summers earlier. Now it was doing double duty as a tomb. At its head we placed a cardboard grave marker with "Ichabod Crane" and 1776-1805 inscribed on it in magic marker (I had recently read a *Classics Illustrated* version of *The Legend of Sleepy Hollow*). The way we had planned it, I would lead guests around and point out the tomb. When I exclaimed, "He died of fright," Sam, clad in a Halloween skeleton costume and mask, would rise out of the trunk and wave his arms around menacingly before sinking back again into the trunk. (The whole show lasted only a minute or two, so he was in no danger of suffocating.)

Tommy was pretty good with a hammer and nails, so he climbed up a ladder and hung my mother's old beige curtains from the rafters to break up the space. When our next-door neighbor, Kevin Schmidt, popped his head into the garage to see what we were doing, I got an idea and looked around. There was an old chain in one corner of the garage, near a bald tire.

"Here, you can rattle this," I told Kevin.

"Can I howl too?" Kevin asked.

"Sure," said Tommy. "You can howl all you want!"

"Think I'll ask my mom if I can take one of her old pots to bang on," Kevin mused. "You know, footsteps . . ."

I forget whose idea it was to place a red devil's mask over the utility light by the garage door, but it was a good one. By jerking a long string, Tommy could turn the light on and off, so it would seem like the devil had glowing eyes.

Tommy had another idea.

"I think we should give out prizes," he announced. "Anyone who comes to the show gets a chance to win a prize."

"What'll the prize be?" I asked.

"How about a yoyo? I have a couple at home that I haven't played with much. Or maybe a fake snake? I got it. The fake snake can be the grand prize—the g.p., and the yoyo can be the grand grand prize—the g.g.p!"

"The g.g.p?" I had to laugh at Tommy's nomenclature. "Sounds good," I said. Tommy ran home and back, and brought the yoyo and the fake snake. He carefully draped the snake over the mock tombstone.

While we were still setting up, my father poked his head inside. Fortunately, he parked the family car on the driveway in the summer, never in the garage.

"What's going on?" he asked. Evidently my mother hadn't bothered to tell him.

"Setting up a spook show," I replied.

He frowned. That was his default expression. Like Tommy's father, he wasn't in the best of health. He had already had one heart attack before we moved to New Jersey from Pittsburgh several years earlier. I used to worry a lot that he'd have another one. His face would get red with the slightest exertion, and he often coughed. He had a heart doctor, but this was before they did bypasses, so there wasn't much doctors could do if you had arteries blocked from decades of cholesterol.

"Well, don't get into anything," he growled, and left. I was relieved. You never knew how my father would react to things. If he was in a particularly bad mood, he could be quite nasty.

A day later the spook show began. The neighborhood kids had this amazed look on their faces as I guided them around the garage. Tommy switched the devil light on and off and on via the long string. Sam popped out of the steamer trunk on cue, while Kevin made hellacious noises behind the back curtain. Some of the kids were so impressed that they paid a dime to see the show again. I forget who won the prizes. All told we made a few bucks. But the biggest payoff was entertaining the kids. We lived in a development where you had to get an adult to drive you places. The spook show was something we kids accomplished on our own.

A few months later, I learned that Tommy's dad had died. The radiation treatments—which had probably been very crude—hadn't helped at all.

The next summer, my father suffered another heart attack and collapsed late one evening at the dining room table. Ever the conscientious metallurgist, he had been outlining some project for work one night on a yellow legal pad when he was stricken. He was dead by the time the ambulance arrived.

Neither Tommy nor I ever talked to each other about our fathers' deaths. We continued to play catch and sometimes "kick the can" in the street as if nothing had happened. Mrs. Del Vecchio still shouted "Tommy," and he still replied "what-y." Sometimes Mrs. Del Vecchio would drive Tommy, Joanne Muhlbacher, and me to a roller skating rink in Glassboro. It was fun going around and around the rink to the corny music. Although Tommy was a much better skater than Joanne or me, I don't recall him ever making fun of our tendency to hug the wall. About a year later, Mrs. Del Vecchio sold their house and the family moved away—as I recall, they were going back to live with Tommy's grandmother. That was the last I heard of them, until recently.

Writing all this in the warm glow of nostalgia compelled me to look up Tommy Del Vecchio on the Internet. It would be an understatement to say what I found put a different slant on my warm memories. Staring out from a mug shot taken in Florida was Tommy. I was sure it was he. He was the right age, and he had the same blue-green, close-set eyes, short nose, and round face. Only he was older and grizzled and looked to be a barfly like someone out of Charles Bukowski.

According to the news story—which was from a local website in Florida—Tommy had made drunken advances toward a nine-year-old girl on a public beach—telling her she was beautiful and asking her if she and her adult cousin, who was also present, wanted to go home with him. He had also tripped the nine year old and either deliberately or by accident flicked cigarette ash at her. When the girl and her cousin threatened to call the cops on him, he hurried away. But based on his description, the police tracked him down and arrested him on charges of felony child abuse.

The article went on to say that he had a prior arrest for "defrauding an innkeeper." Amazed, I continued looking through the entries on Thomas Del Vecchio and came across more mug shots. In each one, he looked angry, hard, and defiant. He looked aggrieved—like the kind of guy who felt as if everyone else had something that he didn't, and he wanted what they had. Evidently, he had been in trouble with the law more than once. His rap sheet, though not lengthy, included grand theft auto.

I printed out a copy of the article and showed it to my brother Sam.

"Do you think that's Tommy?" I asked him.

He stared at it. "Yes," he said. He couldn't stop staring at the mug shot. I guess, like me, he was trying to see the child in the man.

This two-bit criminal was one of my dear childhood friends! We still had a photo of him in the family album. In it, he and Sam and Kevin Schmidt's little sister Pamela are grinning for the camera. Tommy has by far the largest grin.

ZIP

I was sitting in the recreation room watching TV on a Sunday afternoon with my father. I was about nine years old. I don't remember where my mother was, probably performing one of the tedious chores that seemed to be her lot in life. As the credits rolled and the movie *Pal Joey* began, my father suddenly turned to me and said, "You can't watch this. It's for adults only."

"Why?" I asked, but he gave no answer. He simply repeated that the movie was for adults. He seemed sort of smug when he said it, as if he knew something I didn't. I was pissed. Even at this early date, I adored beautiful actresses. I knew enough to know that there was no violence in this movie. Nor was it a horror movie that would be likely to give me nightmares. Storming out of the recreation room, I ran up to my bedroom, slammed the door, threw myself on my bed, and sobbed bitterly. I felt that my father was denying me a pleasure that he was intent on enjoying himself. I vaguely realized that that pleasure was intimately connected to the female sex. I thought my father was being selfish.

Although *Pal Joey*, which started Frank Sinatra, Rita Hayworth, and Kim Novak was somewhat racy for its time, the average soap opera today has far more sex in it. In the movie, Rita Hayworth plays an ex-stripper who marries a rich man and is then widowed. Frank Sinatra, who plays Joey Evans, a second-rate singer and notorious womanizer, wants her to finance a nightclub that he will call Chez Joey. The only catch is that Joey finds himself attracted to a beautiful young chorus girl played by Kim Novak. If Joey pursues Kim Novak's character, he loses the club deal.

Back when I was a kid I didn't understand why my father didn't want me to watch *Pal Joey*. Now of course I do. My father wanted to enjoy the sexy women all by himself. I guess that he, a married man with a heart condition and seven kids, wanted to imagine himself as Pal Joey, a carefree bachelor whose major problem in life was choosing between Rita Hayworth and Kim Novak. Watching this movie was my father's escape. Having me—a product of his desire—in the room while he was watching it would have destroyed the illusion.

My father hadn't a clue about my budding sexuality. Because one of my childhood friends was a boy named Randy, my father would sometimes sing a lyric, "Randy, is a minister handy?" which was a variation on the song "Mandy" from the movie, *White Christmas*. The assumption was that my pal Randy would become my boyfriend. Even back then, before I really knew I was a lesbian, this assumption used to gall me. Randy was a bright and loyal friend, and I certainly appreciated him for sharing his *Batman* comic books with me, but I found the idea of marrying him decidedly unappealing.

Two years later, my father died of a massive heart attack, years before I could have announced my lesbianism to him. Just out of curiosity, I recently watched Rita Hayworth's big song and dance number "Zip" in *Pal Joey* on Youtube.com. In it she references her stripper past as she vamps across the stage making references to the German philosopher, Schopenhauer, the political commentator, Walter Lippmann, and the burlesque house operator, Minsky. But the only thing Hayworth takes off as she prances about the stage is her long white gloves. She also does a bit of flirtatious posturing with some long white embellishments that hang off her dress. That's the number my father didn't want me to see? Shit.

Or perhaps it was another *Pal Joey* number, in which Kim Novak's character takes a dare and strips down to her bustier and a little skirt thing. Before she can go any further, Sinatra, who has the hots for her, grows squeamish and tells her to go to her dressing room and put her clothes on. He has realized that she's a nice girl at heart, nice and young enough for him to marry. Not old (thirty-nine!) and used up like Rita Hayworth. (By the way, Sinatra was three years older than Hayworth when *Pal Joey* was released.)

When I came of age, I used to go to lesbian bars in Philly. Sometimes the bars would feature strippers. These young women stripped down to pasties and a g-string in front of an admiring, if not exactly lustful, all-female audience. The strippers had luscious bodies. I wonder what my father would have thought if he knew I had seen them.

Like father, like daughter? Or, all his efforts, for naught. That's what happens when a parent dies young. You just never know.

GREAT DEPRESSION

I was eight years old and knew I was in trouble when the screw fell out of the right hinge of my eyeglasses. In desperation I got down on my hands and knees and scoured the sidewalk for the screw, but I couldn't find it. But necessity is the mother of invention. So what I did was take a pin from my mother's sewing box and put it in the hinge in place of the screw. I bent the pin so its sharp end wouldn't cut my face.

So here I am walking around with a pin holding the right earpiece to my glasses. Stupidly, I hoped my mother wouldn't notice.

Unfortunately, she noticed. We were standing in the living room of my family's split-level home.

"What is this???!!" she asked, her voice rising as she plucked my glasses from my face. "What did you do to your glasses???!!!" she shrieked.

"The screw fell out . . . I couldn't find it," I managed to explain.

She got a mad gleam in her eyes.

"Taking a pin . . . !!!" My mother was simply outraged that I had allowed the screw to fall out. It was just one more aggravating thing for her to deal with. She, who couldn't cope.

I began to blubber and ran to my room. My mother ranted for a few more minutes, then quieted down and began preparing dinner. Meatloaf.

In actuality, a trip to the local Kmart would have fixed the glasses. As I later noticed, they sold eyeglass repair kits, complete with tiny screwdriver and replacement screws, at checkouts. They cost about a buck or two. After my mother recovered her sanity, that was probably just what we did. But I forget that part.

Another "situation": It was night time, a Saturday night in summer, and my younger brother Sam was running around the recreation room in his bare feet. He stepped on a thumbtack, and it went into his foot. I don't know where the thumbtack came from . . . probably from a bulletin board that my older brother Bob used to display the old postcards he collected. I don't recall Sam shouting in pain, though he must have. I do remember my mother shrieking at him for stepping on the thumbtack. It was like Armageddon going off in our rec room. Even the cat ran and hid. How foolish of Sam to have an accident! Now my mother would have to take him to the doctor, and he would have to get a tetanus shot. It was just too much to deal with.

My mother had some insight into her condition. "I have bad nerves," she used to say in her quieter moments. But she never apologized. I guess she felt that cooking and cleaning for us all those years was enough. It's a good question: how many dinners cooked and cookies baked and toilets scrubbed compensate for terrifying your children?

My mother had been taking the tranquilizer Meprobamate throughout my childhood, even when my father was still alive. However, it didn't seem to help much. Sometimes she'd tell me that she hadn't slept all night. When she had a run of insomnia, she'd let her short gray hair get greasy and lank. Other times she'd tell him how badly her head hurt. She'd sit at the breakfast table with her hand on the side of her head, a crucified look on her face. I felt bad for her, but what could I do?

Finally she had to be hospitalized for depression. A staff psychiatrist at Underwood Memorial Hospital put her on Paxil. The psychiatrist wanted her to come in for therapy, but she refused.

"What good would that do?" she said. She wanted to be self-reliant, like her immigrant parents had been. Talk therapy was self-indulgent . . . something for rich people. But drugs were okay, under certain circumstances. I know that a lot of people frown on antidepressants these days, but Paxil definitely helped my mother. Gone were the depressive lows, and the anxiety abated somewhat, too.

She joined a senior citizen group at her local church and went on bus trips to the Atlantic City casinos, which she seemed to enjoy. She mellowed, somewhat. Besides, Sam and I were out of the house by now. She couldn't shriek at us the way she used to, although she still did tee off on Bob sometimes, who was developmentally disabled and who would always live at home.

Years later, I was sitting in a board meeting of a local theater company, to which I belonged. Someone asked me to perform a task for the company. I was to contact local media and try to arrange publicity for the company. My lack of confidence must have shown.

"You get a haunted look on your face," my friend Gina later told me. Gina was the president of the company. She was the first and so far the only person to ever say that to me.

Gina is one of the few people I know whose mother wasn't a victim. Gina's mother went to college and then to law school. She eventually became a family court judge. A judge!

My mother had wanted to go to college, but her mother wanted her to work and help support the family, so that was just what she did. This was during the 1930s . . . during the Great Depression. My mother loved literature. When she was a girl, she walked miles to check works by Charles Dickens out of the public library in Sheridan. She told us that she loved walking "up to Sheridan," as if the walk itself put her on a different plane of being. She loved *David Copperfield* and *Great Expectations* and all of those humongous 19th century Victorian novels. She even read Thackeray's *Vanity Fair*. She would have excelled as an English major in college. Instead she worked in an office for a time, adding up columns of numbers. Then she got married to my father, a metallurgist for the Navy, and had seven kids. My younger brother Sam and I were the last two. We lived with her after our father died of a heart attack. The other kids, except for Bob, were out of the house by that time, either going to college or married or working.

One sunny day in April when I was seventeen years old, I got a fat letter in the mail from Vassar College. I opened the letter, read it, and then went to tell my mother what it said. She was out in the back yard hanging clothes.

"I got accepted by Vassar," I said. "They're giving me nearly a full scholarship."

My mother looked at me. She didn't look pleased. She looked annoyed.

"Good," she said. "Why don't you help me hang these clothes?"

I did so.

Anne Taintor is a writer/artist who adds witty captions to 1950s-style images that look as if they could have appeared in the *Ladies Home Journal*. In one of her books there's a picture of a 1950s-style housewife serving dinner. The caption reads something like this: "Pot roast, with a side dish of resentment."

That housewife was my mother to a T.

WHEN I LIKED COUNTRY

A long time ago I liked country music. The man who fostered my appreciation was a young English instructor I had in college whom I shall call John Fredericks. John grew up on a ranch outside of Stockton, California. As far as English professors go, he was rather unusual. He was a cowboy with a Ph.D. from Yale. I wouldn't call him macho per se, but he wore cowboy boots and dipped Copenhagen snuff, which he spit out into paper cups that fell over and stained the interior of his white Volkswagen Beetle. He was too intellectually sophisticated to be comfortable with the sophistries of cowboy life, but he knew men who were, and was comfortable around them. And of course, he had a warm spot for country music, especially bluegrass and the outlaw sub-genre most famously interpreted by Waylon Jennings and Willie Nelson. Despite his Ivy League pedigree, I believe that John fancied himself an outlaw. I got the sense that he was somewhat embarrassed about teaching at a formerly women's college. It wasn't exactly a "manly" occupation. In fact, it was something that the men he had grown up around would have made lewd jokes about. "All that pussy," they would have said.

It wasn't a coincidence that John was my freshman year English instructor. I had signed up for his section of English 105 based on its description in the list of intro courses I had been sent over the summer. The theme of John's section was "The Isolato" in literature. According to Dictionary.com, an *isolato* is a person who is "out of sympathy" with his or her time. The books and short stories to be read in John's section were Fitzgerald's *The Great Gatsby*, Faulkner's *Light in August*, Melville's "Bartleby the Scrivener" and "Benito Cereno," "The Open Boat," and "The Blue Hotel" by Stephen Crane, Nathaniel West's *The Day of the Locust*, and Samuel Beckett's *Murphy*. All were about people out of sympathy with their time, or any time, for that matter. The term *isolato* certainly described me. Although I didn't know it at the time (or didn't *want* to know it), I was a lesbian. I lived in a household with my chronically depressed mother; my father had died of a heart attack when I was eleven . . . just keeled over one night at the dining room table. I was a brainy girl who was growing up in a blue collar subdivision in southern New Jersey. You had to have a car to get anywhere, and I didn't have a car. Living there was so stultifying, it felt like chewing lead.

Fortunately, I scored a 780 on the verbal section of the SAT and won a full, or nearly full scholarship to an elite college. Going to college was a whole 'nuther ball game. The bright-eyed young people, the lovely campus were an embarrassment of riches. Besides, it didn't take me long to view John Fredericks with awe. I had never met anyone like him, probably because living out in rural South Jersey, I had never met anyone. John was broad-chested, and muscular, having been a wrestler in prep school and college, with springy hair the color of a copper penny, a strong jaw, and piercing blue eyes. He was unlike all the other men in the English department. I wouldn't call them "effete" Easterners because that's way too much of a stereotype, but it's unlikely they would have been at home on a ranch.

In addition to the fact that I found John pleasing to look at, it seemed we shared a taste in literature. As I was soon to find out, we both liked Herman Melville's and Flannery O'Connor's short stories, Raymond Chandler's novels, and Norman Mailer's political writing. John was also a fiction writer, and encouraged his students to write creatively. "You are a writer," he wrote on the first creative nonfiction paper I wrote for him. I wasn't used to getting praise from anyone, especially not a man like John. I lapped up his praise like whiskey. I was delighted when I got a note telling me I had been accepted into Narrative Writing for my sophomore year. One had to compete against other students to get in. They didn't accept just anyone. John Fredericks taught the class.

Autumn was a beautiful time of year at college. The fall foliage was vivid along the Hudson, the air crisp and electric. The campus was like how F. Scott Fitzgerald described Princeton in *This Side of Paradise:* romantic and gothic, only with more hills and taller pine trees. Screw spring: I have always found autumn to be the most romantic time of year. Perhaps it's the contrast between the dying year and the demands of the flesh. Van Morrison's "Moondance" was a song of the moment. As the days grew shorter and fall meandered into the holiday season, I felt myself becoming more and more infatuated with John Fredericks.

During our last narrative writing class before Christmas break, John brought a jug of red wine to class. My townhouse mates and I had already downed a celebratory screwdriver or two before I came to class. When I drank the wine, the walls of our classroom started spinning. Just as John was handing out the course evaluation forms, I heaved the contents of my stomach onto the conference table in front of me. My classmates must have been shocked. John later joked that this was my commentary on his teaching. Later, after two classmates, Karen and Marissa, assisted me in getting cleaned up in the ladies' room, I walked back to class. It sounds corny to say, but I looked at John and he looked at me. The ice had been broken. We went out to a roadhouse after class in the company of another writing student, Todd Ashton. I don't know exactly how or why, but both of us wound up spending the night at John's apartment. Although nothing happened beyond lots of boozy talk, a tacit understanding had been reached between John and me. That was the beginning of our "affair," if you could even call it that.

As I later learned, I was one of several of John's student and faculty girlfriends. He phoned me sometimes when he was going on a binge. He'd get drunk and couldn't stop. He worried a lot about getting tenure . . . it was a difficult thing to do at an elite college. One night he called me at the off-campus house I shared with four other students and asked me to take a cab over to his place. He also instructed me to pick up a bottle of gin at a liquor store that was on the way. This was back when the drinking age was eighteen in New York State. I did as instructed. I had never bought a bottle of hard liquor before. I was happy to, although I knew that John's drinking was self-destructive. He had hinted on several occasions that alcoholism ran in his family.

On one particularly memorable Sunday afternoon in the spring, I saw John arrested for drunk driving. A few minutes earlier, I had been in the car with him, but I had insisted on getting out when I saw the car weave over the white medial strip. I hadn't wanted to see myself smashed against the dash board or wrapped around a telephone pole. As I trudged down the road, I saw the cops pick John up a little way up the road and put him in their patrol car. John saw me watching him. He frowned at me with his boozy, bloodshot eyes, as if I had betrayed him.

Evidently the college administration was understanding, since John wound up getting tenure despite this misadventure. They hadn't known a student had been involved, since I hadn't told them. Things were pretty lax back then, as far as instructors having relationships with students went. Perhaps instructors who were creative writers were given a little more leeway. Consider: John Berryman, Robert Lowell, Anne Sexton, John Cheever, and other literary maniacs were *au courant*. Then again, John wound up marrying another of his student girlfriends, so even now, I can't say that faculty/student relationships are all bad.

As I said before, John liked country music, and, encouraged by him, I developed a taste for it. I liked Waylon Jennings, Bill Monroe, and Loretta Lynn. I even liked Tammy Wynette, though even then I took that crap about standing by your man with a grain of salt. A little later on, I became intrigued by the work of storyteller Tom T. Hall, who wrote the song "Harper Valley PTA" for Jeannie C. Riley. I fancied that I might be a popular writer too one day. That was before I realized that writing poetry was my strong suit. The words *popular* and *poet* don't exactly go hand in hand.

My relationship with John ended predictably enough. One day, in my junior year, I found out from another student that John wasn't going to be at school next year, and that he was, in fact, going to be teaching at another college. He hadn't even bothered to tell me. On the other hand, from his point of view, why should he? We weren't really going together. I was just someone he liked to have around once in a while to assuage his loneliness, like a pet dog or cat. I came in handy when another of his women dumped him. In that, I was sort of like a utility player on a baseball team. I allowed myself to get into this situation because I was naïve and didn't ask questions. I was grateful for John's attention. I was trying very hard not to be a lesbian. You might say I had very little self-esteem. Nonetheless, I took John's apparent lack of interest in me hard. Not that the sex, the few times that we had it, was ever right for me. How could it have been? I was a lesbian.

All this happened over thirty years ago. But a recent visit to my niece's house in Nashville brought it all back home. After attending a blue grass concert and touring the Hank Williams exhibit at the Country Music Hall of Fame, I reflected on what knowing John Fredericks had meant to me in terms of clarifying what I value. Like John, I value people who are able to give a voice to loneliness, as Hank Williams had done. I value connection with the land, and wish I lived somewhere other than southern New Jersey. I have respect for hard-working people and a mistrust of technology. People who can't be alone, who constantly manipulate their smart phones in public give me the creeps.

I also appreciate conciseness of expression. Poets like Robert Frost and Kay Ryan, who put things simply and profoundly, move me. If I could, I would own land out west somewhere. I would live in some place with a beautiful view of mountains and enough room to keep horses. In the early 1990s, I attended a writers' conference in western Montana, near Flathead Lake, and I thought it was heaven. "It would be fine to die," I thought while gazing at mountains like strong shoulders, "if I could merge into this."

However, getting such a place seems unlikely. I would have to earn much, much more from my writing than I have hitherto done. But hope, as they say, springs eternal. By way of goading myself to work harder, I sometimes go on the computer and check out what John Frederick's been up to. He's published three fairly well-received novels and edited a couple of nonfiction books. He's retired from teaching now and is probably set for life. I have to keep working. My consolation is that I know I am a better poet and nonfiction writer than John is a novelist. One day in his office in the English department, he told me that I had major league literary talent. About that, at least, he was right.

Romance

Recently I was walking through "Bargain Book Warehouse," a store filled with discounted books located in a nearby strip mall. The books were publisher's overstocks: the unwanted stepchildren of the publishing industry. When I passed by the tables heavily laden with discounted paperback romances, I recalled how I used to heave armfuls of these books into stinking trash compactors in Kmarts throughout southern New Jersey.

This was back when I was working for the Reader's Market, a division of the now-defunct Waldenbooks, which was in turn a subsidiary of Kmart. In addition to managing an expanded book department at the Clementon Kmart, I would go around to other Kmarts and service their smaller paperback book sections. Servicing their book departments invariably meant tearing the covers off of all the paperbacks that hadn't sold after a period of a month or so and throwing the books out to make room for the new titles that were shipped every week. Since very few of the titles sold all that well, this amounted to heaps of books. I had to sort the torn covers and return them to the publishers, so the store could get credit for all the books that didn't sell. During the two years I worked for Reader's Market, I must have thrown out thousands of paperbacks.

A large percentage of the books I put on shelves and later trashed were romances. Working with this merchandise was very alienating for me as a lesbian. I had absolutely no interest in Harlequin romances or those titles known as bodice rippers featuring scantily clad men and women in period costume. In truth, I rather despised the women who bought them. I knew it was wrong for me to despise them. But did their desire have to take such cheesy form? All pinks and purples, the book covers throbbed like engorged genitalia. And the prose was so hackneyed, so devoid of literary value, it made Stephen King sound like Proust. I guess the woman who bought these books weren't satisfied with their mates, if they had any. Then again, when is anyone ever completely satisfied with one's mate? I mean sexually. The wives read romance novels while the husbands whacked off to *Playboy* (this was before streaming Internet porn). Freud had it right: civilization *is* discontent.

Not that lesbians are much better. But at least with lesbians, you know that both parties tend to be romantic. Are there lesbian romances? Yes, there are. In fact, they're a growing market segment, although you'll probably never find them on Kmart shelves. From what I've seen, they're escapist nonsense too. They have titles like *Passion's Bright Fury* and *Wasted Heart*. I don't read them. Through bitter experience, I've come to believe that desire is the opiate of the people.

Let me tell you—in one of the Kmarts I serviced, I became attracted to a woman who worked in receiving. She was a big-boned, lusty-looking brunette with a Southern drawl and an air of vulnerability that belied her Junoesque stature. Her name was Jeannie. After repeated trips to this store, I got to know Jeannie a little. She used to scrawl "Book Lady" with a flourish on all the incoming cartons of books meant for me. She was originally from Raleigh, North Carolina. Her sad tale was that she had been married twice, both times to disappointing men. She had kids—two nice-looking teenagers who worked part-time for Kmart while attending high school—but was now divorced.

One day as I pushed a shopping cart full of paperbacks through receiving to the trash compactor, I heard Jeannie singing along with the song that was playing over the store intercom, "Hungry Eyes."

"I've got hungry eyes." Jeannie was looking at me as she sang this, slightly off key. I could feel that she was mildly attracted to me. Or maybe she was just whiling away the monotony of her job with a fleeting sexual fantasy. As things turned out, not long after I first set eyes on her,

Jeannie and I both transferred to the newly opened Plum Hill Kmart—she in receiving and I as a sporting goods/ automotive manager. Ever hopeful, I took this as a sign that we were meant to be together.

Dave Tilden—a district manager for Kmart at the time— had unintentionally aided and abetted our relationship by recruiting me to be a departmental manager at the new store.

"You're doing a very good job as Reader's Market manager," he told me as we sat at an orange plastic table in the Kmart grill. "So which department at Plum Hill would you like to manage?"

"Sports/auto," I said, even though I knew this position meant working a forty-eight-hour week instead of a forty-hour one. Selling fishing rods and spark plugs paid better than selling paperbacks.

The new job did prove to be a lot of hard work. I wasn't naturally an organized person, and it took me a while to get the hang of managing two stockrooms full of everything from automotive batteries to deer urine. But I was happy that Jeannie was back there in receiving. Although she for the most part was indifferent to my efforts to get to know her better, we did go out to dinner a few times at Mikey's—a restaurant and bar across the street from the store. This was when we both had to work until ten pm— closing time. With the Phillies game on in the background at Mikey's, Jeannie told me about her mom.

"She used to feed us beans while she ate steak," Jeannie said with disgust. Hers sounded like a very rough childhood. "I guess that's why I like food and kitchen stuff so much," she added. Jeannie knew good pots and pans when she saw them. Not cheap Kmart stuff.

"What's the difference?" I asked her. She looked at me as if I had two heads.

"Good pots and pans *cook* better," she said. "*And* they last longer."

Since we were on the topic of cooking, I told Jeannie about the time Martha Stewart autographed one of her cookbooks for me and about fifty other Reader's Market managers. The book signing occurred at a Reader's Market managers' meeting in Westchester, New York. This was back when Martha was just making a name for herself as a doyenne of domesticity. I told Jeannie what Martha had written in my copy of Martha Stewart's *Quick Cook* book: "To Ruth, Be entertaining, always. Martha Stewart." This was before Martha got convicted of insider trading and sent to prison.

Jeannie was mildly impressed by my name-dropping Martha, but not enough to be interested in me. She did tell me an interesting thing, though. She said that Paul, one of the assistant managers at our store, had propositioned her.

"Paul? He's engaged!" I replied. *Not only that,* I thought to myself, *but he's twenty years younger than you.*

Again Jeannie looked at me as if I had two heads.

"That don't mean much these days," she opined.

I had actually met Paul's fiancée. He had introduced her to me one day while I was putting up a new fishing display. Her name was Karla. It was clear that she had stars in her eyes when she looked at Paul. She seemed like a very nice young woman. Now that I knew what a dog Paul was, I felt sorry for her. She didn't know what she was getting into.

Secretly, I was rather pleased that Paul considered Jeannie attractive. It proved to me that I didn't have poor taste in being attracted to her. However, she had no romantic use for either Paul or me. She had her heart set on a butch woman who worked as a computer systems trainer for Kmart. As things turned out, a few months later she and this woman went off to Phoenix together when Kmart transferred the woman out there. A year after that, they broke up, and Jeannie moved back to South Jersey and once again started working at the Plum Hill Kmart. This time she settled in Bordentown, New Jersey, about forty-five minutes north of Plum Hill, off of Rt. 295. A few nights, when we both had to work until ten pm and then come in at eight the next morning, Jeannie stayed over my apartment rather than commute back home. Nothing happened. She slept on my sofa bed in the living room, while I slept in my bed in the bedroom. I was disappointed, but at least it was nice having someone with whom to watch the crimes, fires, and accidents on the eleven o'clock news.

So Jeannie and I never did get together. She just didn't like me that much, physically. Although she was a tall, Amazonian woman who could probably knock you into next week if she tried, she took the sheets in bed. A few months later, the Plum Hill Kmart went out of business. I remember the day that Dave Tilden called the management team into his office.

"This store has never made a nickel in profit," Dave told us. I admired the fact that he was forthright. It seemed that the Plum Hill Kmart was somewhat off the beaten track. Rather than being located on a major thoroughfare such as Rt. 70 or Rt. 38, it sat at the end of a road that not everyone was familiar with. In fact, many Plum Hill residents hadn't realized there was a Plum Hill Kmart until they noticed our going-out-of-business ad in the local papers. By now Dave held a jaundiced view of Kmart Corporation.

"I'd rather stick pins in my eyes than call headquarters," he said.

After the hubbub of the store closing, Jeannie relocated back to North Carolina and began working for a Kmart down there. I felt it was high time to put my BA in English to use, so I turned down Dave's offer to manage at another Kmart. Instead I went to work for a book distribution company and then got a job as an apprentice teacher with the School District of Philadelphia. I went to Saint Joseph's University after the school day to earn my certification and master's in education.

I don't know what was more grueling—working for Kmart or teaching in inner-city schools. I used to joke that retail would be fun were it not for the customers. I sometimes thought education would be fun, without the kids. I now teach part-time at a GED program and write part-time for an educational publishing company. I have written two nonfiction books geared to young adults, which the company has published. I haven't seen Jeannie in seventeen years.

Recently, however, the sight of all those paperback romances laid out upon tables at Bargain Book Warehouse led me to Google her. I found her on Facebook. In her photo, she's standing in a nicely appointed kitchen, a smile on her face. There is a pretty granite kitchen island in front of her and handsome-looking pots and pans behind her. She's put on a little weight. Her hair is dyed a rusty red. She's clearly in her element. I can imagine she eats steak anytime she wants. I didn't bother to "friend" her. I had wasted too much time enamored of her.

Still, knowing Jeannie was one of the better parts of my tenure with Kmart. Our relationship wasn't a romance. But it wasn't bad.

CUTE

My mother died a few years ago, in a nursing home near where she had lived for over fifty years—in Gloucester County, New Jersey. She spent only a month and a half in the nursing home. Before that she had spent three years in an assisted living facility in another town. When she began to have difficulty swallowing even pureed food, the people at the assisted living place advised my brother and me that she needed to be placed in a nursing home. They said that she was choking on her food more and more often during meals. What was not entirely clear to me at the time was that my mother was at the point of aspirating her food. Aspiration occurs when aged throat muscles grow so weak that swallowed food gets into the lungs, inevitably causing infection and death. When death came for my mother, the assisted living people didn't want it to be at their place, on their watch.

So late one winter afternoon, a medical transport van came to take my mother from assisted living to the Willow Valley Nursing Facility. I had already researched Willow Valley via the Internet and found it had gotten good reviews. In fact, it had gotten four stars. Also, I had learned by word-of-mouth that it was a well-run place. Still, of course, the transition was unwelcome. Although my mother was somewhat senile, she knew what was happening. The nursing home was to be the last stop on the road to oblivion. Willow Valley, indeed.

"When are they taking me?" she had asked me the day before.

"Tomorrow," I had told her. There was little time to prepare her emotionally for the transition because a bed had just "opened up" at Willow Valley. You've got to say yes quickly when beds open up in reputable nursing homes. Otherwise, you lose out.

"I'll be here tomorrow, too," I assured her.

By this point, my mother knew the move was inevitable. That didn't mean she liked it. I'll never forget the frightened look in her eyes as she was lifted into the transport van. It was one of those vans that have a lift, so the person being transported never has to get out of her or his wheelchair. It was a frigid evening. It was December. I had dressed my mother warmly in her sweater, knit hat, and red wool coat, but she still looked frail and vulnerable, her white hair reflecting the cold glow of the streetlights.

I had assured her I would follow the van to Willow Valley, and I did. But on the way, we were separated by a red light, and I wound up taking another, slightly longer route. By the time I arrived, the head duty nurse and her assistant were already checking my mother in. This meant, in part, that they were checking her body for bedsores. They didn't want to be held responsible if the assisted living place had let things get out of hand.

"She's so cute!" they were exclaiming. I found this comment a little odd. Here, my mother was ninety-five years old. "Cute" wasn't an adjective I would have used to describe her. Old, decrepit, somewhat senile, nearly deaf and blind, incontinent—yes. But cute?

I tried to look at my mother through their eyes. She was very little, shrunken from what had been an already petite five-foot frame. But she was still a rather pretty woman. She had good bone structure and a pink, unblemished complexion. She had a certain refinement that was hard to describe—a quiet, self-containment that suggested a complex inner life. Plus, she was meek. Always intimidated by authority, she let the nurse and her assistant examine her without saying a word.

"Her skin hasn't broken down," the head nurse Karen assured me after they had put her into bed.

This wasn't exactly news to me. I knew they had taken good care of her at the assisted living place. They had been paid big bucks to do so.

"Oh, she's just so cute!" Karen's assistant Lisa again exclaimed. Before Karen and Lisa left the room, Karen said they would send someone around with a tray of food, since my mother seemed too tired to go to the dining room this evening.

My mother watched from her bed as I unpacked some of her clothes and began to put them away. I had also brought some of the family photos we had displayed at the assisted living place.

"Here's Father," I said, handing her a framed photograph of my father, her husband of thirty years. She held it in her hands. Then she brought it to her lips and kissed it fiercely. After she handed it back to me, I placed it on the nightstand beside her.

I had also brought some photographs of her great-grandchildren—Ona, Roberto, and Braun. These went on the TV stand up above the TV. I knew that my mother, with her macular degeneration, wouldn't be able to see these photos from her wheelchair or bed, but there was nowhere else to put them. I also took out my mother's teddy bear and placed it on a chair. It had been a Christmas gift from my sister, Laura. My mother had asked for it. It seemed a comfort to her in her extreme old age.

A few minutes later, a young red-haired woman came by with a tray of pureed food—mashed potatoes and some kind of pureed meat and a vegetable, plus thickened juice.

As she sat spoon-feeding my mother, the young woman suddenly turned to me and said, "Your mother's so cute!"

I must have looked amused.

"We have some residents around here who are really difficult," the young woman quickly explained. "But your mom seems *darling* . . . so pleasant and easy-going!"

I had to smile at this. My mother had always put her best face forward with strangers. But there had been many times in my youth when she had been anything but darling.

"Not all the time . . ." I began to say.

"Oh, well *everyone's* mother is like that sometimes," countered the young woman.

It was clear she liked taking care of my mother. That was a good thing. It saddened me to watch my mother eat, though. It was so slow, so hard for her. And a few short weeks from now, the food that should be nourishing her would begin getting into her lungs, leading to the inevitable decline and fall.

After a little while, the young woman asked my mother if she had had enough.

My mother nodded.

A few minutes after the young woman left, I kissed my mother and said good-bye. I told her I would visit her again the next day.

"Alright," she agreed. She seemed comfortable—calmly resigned to her new surroundings.

It took me several minutes to find my way out of Willow Valley. I've never had a very good sense of direction, and I found myself wandering down the same corridor more than once—looking for the exit. As I did, I noticed the residents. Although some still seemed in relatively good shape, others were decrepit, with drooping heads and dazed eyes. One woman, whose hair was incongruously black, had a large bandage over her nose and cheek that made her look clownish. Still, she smiled at me as I walked past her for the third time, looking for the exit. She must have thought *I* was demented.

Finally, I did find an exit. It was past the main dining area. As I walked outside into the parking area, past piles of snow, under the cold moon, I decided that there were far worse things to be called than "cute." I guessed the people at Willow Valley had the right idea about my mother. Although they would never know what she had been at her best, they would treat her gently, as if she were a delicate doll.

Since my mother had to go, as everyone must, I supposed she might as well do it here.

THE PHILLIES, DICK ALLEN, AND ME

It was the morning of September 7, 1964, and I was sick with excitement about attending my first Phillies games: a Labor Day doubleheader against the Dodgers. This doubleheader took place two weeks before the ten-game losing streak that would cost the Phils the pennant. Sometimes I think their monumental '64 collapse scarred me for life. Other times I think it taught me the meaning of life.

Let me backtrack a bit: before spring, 1964, baseball didn't make sense to me. I couldn't understand the unique geometry of the game . . . the diamond path around the bases, the balls and strikes, why some balls hit into the field were considered hits while others were outs. Understanding baseball was like fiddling with binoculars—after some adjustments, suddenly a clear image swims into view.

My love of baseball came as a surprise to my older sister Laura.

"Ruth likes baseball because she wants to win Steve's approval," I heard her sagely telling my mother. Steve was my older brother. Laura was a clinical psychologist who took her marching orders from Freud. A naturally girly girl, she believed in traditional sex roles. Accordingly, the idea that a girl could love baseball for its own sake was beyond her ken.

"Why don't you play with the little girls?" she'd ask me when I'd come home all grimy from playing baseball with the boys. The implication was that I was doing something wrong in hanging with the boys. I guess in her mind I was upsetting the Freudian apple cart. At that time I didn't have enough worldly wisdom to tell her that it wasn't playing ball *with the boys* I loved so much as simply playing ball.

I also loved watching baseball on TV. Steve and I watched Jim Bunning's Father's Day perfect game against the Mets on our black- and- white Olympic while sipping homemade lemonade in our recreation room. Steve, who would be going away to college in the fall, was a font of baseball lore.

"This will be the first perfect game in the National League in eighty-four years," he enthused. "Don Larsen was the last major leaguer to pitch one, in the 1956 World Series."

Steve also clued me in to the fact that players on the pitcher's team weren't supposed to talk about the possibility of a perfect game. That would be jinxing it.

We both idolized Jim Bunning, a veteran who had come to the Phillies in an off-season trade with the Detroit Tigers. Bunning was six-foot-four and lanky. After the ball left his hand, the momentum of his sidearm delivery nearly caused him to fall off the mound. His best pitch was a devastating slider. When Bunning struck out John Stephenson to end the game in the long shadows of Shea Stadium, we shouted so loudly that my mother came to the top of the stairs to see what was happening.

"That's wonderful!" she said when we told her.

It was icing on the cake when Bunning took a bow on the Ed Sullivan Show that night. To see a Philadelphia Phillie recognized on national TV was as rare as the proverbial hen's teeth.

Steve was no fair weather Phillies fan. He had begun following the team in 1961, when they lost twenty-three games in a row, still a major league record.

"I just wondered when they'd ever win a game," he later told me. After 1961, he had witnessed the slow arc of the Phillies' rise to respectability. One big reason they were lousy for much of the 1950s and the early 1960s was that when other teams were signing players like Jackie Robinson and Roy Campanella and Willie Mays and Hank Aaron and Ernie Banks, the Phillies adamantly weren't.

Phillies owner Bob Carpenter primly explained, "I'm not opposed to Negro players. But I'm not going to hire a player of any color or nationality just to have him on the team." Evidently he thought he would be doing black ballplayers a big favor by signing them to a Phillies contract. Those Negroes . . . they're just such poor athletes!

In 1957, a full ten years after Jackie Robinson made his Major League debut, the Phillies signed a black journeyman by the name of John Kennedy. When he failed to distinguish himself, they released him and hired a few more mediocre black players . . . mostly from outside the United States.

By the early 1960s, however, Carpenter had seen the light long enough to sign a black *phenom* named Richie Allen. By 1964 Allen, a clear Rookie of the Year favorite, was not only hitting tape measure homeruns, but was among the league leaders in batting average. The rest of the team was much improved also. Power-hitting right fielder Johnnie Callison had hit a three-run homerun to win the All-Star Game for the National League. On the mound, right-handed ace Jim Bunning was on his way to nineteen victories, while fire-balling Chris Short stood second only to Sandy Koufax among National League lefthanders. Managing them was Gene Mauch, the "Little General." Mauch's knowledge of the game was formidable, as was his temper. After one loss, he famously upset a tableful of food in the clubhouse, splattering gravy on outfielder Wes Covington's suit.

I couldn't wait to see these Phillies in person. I was going along with Steve and his best friend, Ed Patterson.

Getting to the game, however, would take some doing.

"Are you sure it's *safe* to go to the stadium?" my mother asked Steve. She was worried because a race riot had broken out in the vicinity of the ballpark just a week earlier over an incident of police harassment. Over 300 people had been injured, 770 had been arrested, and over 200 businesses were damaged or destroyed.

"It'll be broad daylight," Steve reassured her. "There'll be cops around. And the bus lets out right in front of the stadium."

It took about an hour for our bus to wend its way north along Route 45 from our hometown of Mantua, through rural Gloucester County and on into Camden County. As the bus drew closer to the city of Camden, past the soon-to-be shuttered New York Shipyard, the landscape grew ever more urban and ever more depressed. Even then, Broadway in Camden was a chastening sight to a ten-year-old from the sticks. Although the main drag was still lined with businesses, the businesses had that down-at-heels look to them. There were stores that sold furniture that even I could tell was junky, storefronts with grimy, outmoded signs and metal gates, the battered stucco of McCrory's Five and Ten . . . The people, mostly black and Puerto Rican, looked poor and harried. By now white flight was in full swing, eventually transforming Camden from a thriving industrial city to the poorest, most dangerous city in the country. Of course I didn't understand sociology in 1964. All I knew was that to get to the ball game, you had to first go through some "bad" neighborhoods. Our trip then took on the characteristics of a trek.

In downtown Camden, we transferred to the "Phillies Express," a chartered bus that took us over the Ben Franklin Bridge and up Broad Street to North Philadelphia. North Broad Street had been shabby for years. Now—drained by the loss of manufacturing jobs—it was quickly getting worse. As the bus lumbered through city traffic, we seemed to be catching every red light. When the bus turned left onto Lehigh, I could see signs of devastation—burned out businesses, abandoned row houses, junked cars. However, when we finally made it to 21st, I gazed up at the red brick façade of Connie Mack Stadium and was surprised to see that it looked just like a regular building. I don't know what I was expecting—something more sporting? When the Phillies televised home games, they never showed you the outside of Connie Mack. Location, location, location wasn't something the ownership wanted to stress.

As we joined the crowds heading toward the home plate entranceway, grayish men with carts hawked souvenirs—pennants, buttons, balloons, inflatable Phillies dolls . . . anything Phillies. I could well imagine these men had done the same thing for decades, back when the park and neighborhood were in their heyday. With the couple of dollars my mother had given me, I bought a large white button emblazoned with the words "Go Phillies Go!" in red and blue. I still have it.

Many baseball writers have described their first hallowed view of a major league diamond in almost religious terms. Walking through the turnstiles, up the concourse ramp and into the stands was certainly a revelation to me. The emerald field was as immaculate as the stands were grungy. It was a green jewel framed by colorful signs.

As Bruce Kuklick relates in his wonderful history, *To Everything a Season: Shibe Park and Urban Philadelphia: 1909-1976*, Connie Mack Stadium had once been a pleasure palace. When it was christened Shibe Park in 1909—after an A's owner—its concrete and steel construction was state-of-the-art—far more impressive than the Phillies' rinky-dink Baker Bowl. As such, it symbolized the comparative status of the two clubs. Led by manager-part owner Connie Mack, the Philadelphia Athletics were among the elite of the American League, winning five World Championships while the Phillies were barely holding their own in the senior circuit.

But the Athletics fell into decline in the mid-1930s, and for much of the 1940s and 1950s they were in last place or close to it. By this time, the Phillies had moved out of tiny Baker Bowl and had begun sharing Shibe Park with the A's. After the Athletics moved to Kansas City in 1954, the Phillies' millionaire owner Bob Carpenter reluctantly bought the stadium, which had been rechristened Connie Mack, simply because there was no other place for his team to play.

For most of the Phillies' history, their fly-by-night owners had been content to field lousy teams and earn a small profit. As their fans used to say, the team stank despite a sign in the Baker Bowl outfield proclaiming "The Phillies Use Lifebuoy." Now, at least, the ownership appeared committed to winning baseball. As the neighborhood around Connie Mack Stadium became overwhelmingly African-American, poor, and resentful of the white crowds who trespassed on their turf, Philadelphia politicians decided to underwrite the construction of a new stadium in another location. They didn't want to lose the Phillies the way they had lost the Athletics.

Of course, I knew few of these facts in 1964. As Steve, Ed, and I negotiated our way to our seats along the third base line, our shoes stuck to concrete that had been christened many times over with spilled soda and beer. Then we gingerly stepped over a mound of squashed French fries. As we took our seats, sharp-eyed vendors climbed steep steps, bellowing "Hey, Hot Dogs!! Hey Peanuts!!" as if they were calling people by name.

I looked out and took in the outfield . . . the stately, roofed left field bleachers, the bright signage, including the Goldenberger's Peanut Chews sign that looked to me like a giant candy bar in left field, the Ballantine Beer scoreboard topped by the Longines clock, and the high blue wall in right. And then to see the players . . . their crisp white uniforms with red pinstripes and bright red caps, vivid against the deep green grass. You could have your "House That Ruth Built." On this sunny afternoon in early September, Connie Mack Stadium was good enough for me.

I remember the ambience more than the action. I remember that the Phillies won the first game behind the strong pitching of Dennis Bennett and lost the second game behind rookie Rick Wise and veteran Bobby Shantz, who came on in relief. Steve told me that before injuring his arm years earlier, Shantz had won the MVP award as an Athletic. It was nice to see him do well.

That evening, our parents greeted us, relieved that we had returned safely from the wilds of North Philadelphia. As we ate pot roast around the dinner table, I reflected on the games I had seen. Despite the dispiriting second game loss, I felt that the Phillies were still in great shape to win the pennant. They were still something like six games in front. This happy circumstance made the grim thought of starting school the next day that much more tolerable for me.

I won't dwell on the details of the Phillies' collapse because they've already been repeated *ad infinitum*. As every Phillies fan of a certain age knows, the team wound up losing ten straight and finishing second to the St. Louis Cardinals. It was an event both sickening and humiliating.

The next several years were worse for the Phillies from every standpoint. Not only did they fall out of contention, but the racial animosity surrounding them only grew worse. Most black baseball fans didn't follow the Phillies because of the club's reputation for racist hiring practices, while the white fan base resented having to travel to a simmering ghetto to see the games. The fans began venting their spleen on an easy target—Dick Allen, who had let it be known that he no longer wished to be called "Richie." It didn't matter that Allen hit monster homeruns that soared over the Coca Cola script topping the left field grandstand and arced through the humid North Philadelphia night. He wielded a huge, forty-two ounce bat—said to be the heaviest in the majors. That mighty bat was in itself provocation to a certain type of white man.

In 1965, when Allen got into a fistfight with Frank Thomas, who had called him "boy"—the Phillies traded Thomas, but the white fans blamed Allen for being "uppity." My younger brother Sam confirms that when he attended a Phillies game in 1969, fans were shouting racial epithets at Allen. Some even threw batteries and other hard objects at him, forcing him to wear a batting helmet when he played first base. Allen compounded matters, it was said, by behaving "erratically." There were missed practices and rumors of drinking. A white superstar like Mickey Mantle could and did get away with a lot during his playing career. A black superstar couldn't. Not in Philadelphia at least.

Meanwhile, the Phillies front office continued its generally unenlightened ways. In 1966, General Manager John Quinn traded a promising black pitcher, Ferguson

Jenkins, to the Cubs in exchange for two veteran pitchers
. . . Bob Buhl and Larry Jackson—who happened to be
white. Call it kismet: Buhl would win all of six games for
the Phillies before retiring at the end of the 1967 season.
Jackson did better, but retired at the end of 1968 rather
than report to an expansion team. Jenkins, on the other
hand, would win only 284 games in the course of his Hall
of Fame career.

So bad was Philadelphia's reputation around the
National League that when the St. Louis Cardinals traded
Curt Flood and some other players to the Phillies in 1969
for Dick Allen and some other players, Flood refused to
report. He later filed the famous lawsuit that helped pave
the way for free agency. So, one could say that, with the
worst of intentions, Phillies fans ultimately did a good
thing for major league players.

The Phillies played their last game at Connie Mack
Stadium on October 1, 1970. It was an event that novelist
Nathaniel West should have written about—a real day
of the locust type of affair. Even before the last out had
been made, fans began stealing anything they could get
their hands on, including seats that had been bolted to the
concrete. (Even now you can buy wood from these seats
on eBay—two red slats sell for $78.00.) At the time, the
wholesale plundering left a bitter aftertaste. It was like
desecrating a temple, albeit a seedy one. Weeds sprang
up in the field that had once been beautifully tended. The
next year the place caught fire, and in 1976 the twisted
mass of steel and concrete was demolished. Today an
African American church sits on the site.

After the Phillies moved to antiseptic new Veterans
Stadium in South Philadelphia, Steve, Sam, and I used to
shiver through chilly April games there that featured such
luminaries as Billy Champion, Roger Freed, and Joe Lis.
In the later innings, we usually moved up to the box seats
because a lot of fans had left. But, to paraphrase Eliot, in
the Phillies' nadir was their rebirth. A more enlightened
owner, Ruly Carpenter, had taken over from his father.
In 1972 the Phillies finished dead last, but future Hall

of Famer Steve Carlton won twenty-seven games, and sluggers Mike Schmidt and Greg Luzinski began to establish themselves. Together with other talented young players, they would lead the team to years of excellence culminating in the 1980 World Series title. The Phillies' first-ever championship was sweeter for being so long in coming.

So what has following the Phillies taught me? American history, for one thing. Being exposed to Camden and North Philadelphia at an early age made me curious to learn why these places were the way they were. In studying urban America, I learned how patterns of discrimination perpetuated poverty. I also learned about the white flight to the suburbs and the impact of globalization on American manufacturing. On a purely sports-oriented note, I learned that racism hurt the Phillies by making them less competitive. It wasn't luck that led the Cardinals to overtake the Phillies to win the 1964 pennant. It was Gibson and Brock and White and Flood, among others.

On a more elemental level, following the 1964 Phillies made me realize that disaster can occur when you least expect it. Nothing is a sure thing. But there are fleeting moments of bliss, as when a veteran pitcher no-hits the Mets.

My father died in 1966 and so never lived to see the Phillies win the World Series. He wasn't a real baseball fan, but he had worked at the Navy Yard with a lot of South Philly guys, and I think he would have enjoyed the moment. My mother, who lived to be ninety-five, saw two. Each one pleased her. My sister Laura, who moved out to Los Angeles in 1976, has grown much more open-minded about sex roles. She still can't fathom sports, though, and has never been to any kind of professional game. We like to joke that she becomes despondent whenever the Dodgers lose. And my brother Steve still watches every game he can.

After some great seasons with other teams, Dick Allen returned to the Philadelphia area. For years he helped the Phillies with community outreach in urban neighborhoods.

He still does baseball memorabilia shows and appears from time to time at Phillies-sponsored events.

As for me, I like to recall my greatest Phillies memories. There are three. Watching Mike Schmidt hit a homerun into the cold October mist of Montreal, defeating the Expos and sending the Phillies back to the playoffs in 1980.

"He buried it," announcer Andy Musser cried.

When Schmidt crushed that ball, I knew that the ghosts of futility would finally be laid to rest.

And Brad Lidge, after striking out Eric Hinske to win the 2008 World Series, falling to his knees and looking up into the chill Philadelphia night, as fireworks shot off and the electronic Liberty Bell rocked in victory.

And of course, my first sight of the playing field in Connie Mack Stadium that Labor Day long ago. In memory still green.

MESS WITH TEXAS

I've taken three vacations in the past six years, and two of them have been just awful. They weren't awful for the usual touristy reasons—missed connections, bad hotels, passport theft, bad weather and the like. No, the reason my vacations were terrible is that I went with the wrong person. That is, I didn't go with someone I was attracted to. I went with someone whom I tried to be attracted to. If you've ever done that, you probably know that it just doesn't work out.

Let me tell you about my Alaskan cruise. I went with Connie, a perfectly nice middle-aged lesbian. I'm a middle aged lesbian, too. I don't know how nice I am, but I try to be. Connie and I had been going together a little less than a year when we went to Alaska. The thing was . . . I should never have dated Connie in the first place.

The first time I set eyes on her, she was standing in the parking lot of the Holiday Inn on Route 70 in Cherry Hill, New Jersey. She had cropped brown hair, and she was wearing an Oxford-type shirt and men's trousers.

"Oh, no," I thought to myself, "men's trousers." I tend to prefer women who are more traditionally feminine—I guess one would call them "lipstick lesbians." But I was hungry for companionship, so I thought, "What the heck."

Connie had seen my profile on an online dating site and had e-mailed me to ask for a date. She was working in Moorestown as an information systems consultant for a huge defense contractor. She worked in South Jersey during the week and then flew down to her home in San Antonio on Thursday afternoons. I was amazed at her grueling schedule, but she said that it wasn't that uncommon these days.

"There's plenty of us," she told me. Connie had good incentive to commute halfway across the country. She said she made $130 an hour. This was about what I made in an entire day, working as a freelance educational writer.

"Isn't it kind of strange being a liberal lesbian working for a defense contractor?" I asked her over dinner at an Indian restaurant.

"Oh, I don't work for the weapons side of the business," she assured me. "I work for the procurement side."

"But you're still working for a defense contractor," I thought to myself. On the other hand, who was I to be judgmental? My father worked as a metallurgist for the U.S. Navy for thirty-five years. You might say that my upbringing was paid for by the military-industrial complex.

As we continued to talk, I decided that Connie had a nice personality. I was also intrigued by the fact that she was from Texas. I had never met anyone, gay or straight from the Lone Star State. She had that Texas twang, though since she had lived in California for a while, it wasn't too pronounced.

As we kept chatting, I learned that Connie liked baseball and reading about dead presidents. That was funny . . . so did I. Since she had lived in San Francisco for a number of years, her favorite team was the Giants.

"I can't stand Barry Bonds," I opined.

Connie shrugged. "In San Francisco we just say, 'that's Barry being Barry.'"

As the evening wore on, the thought occurred to me that I should try not to be turned off by superficial things such as personal style. My pattern was to be attracted to women who weren't emotionally available. My therapist had suggested that this was because I had had to care so much for my mother, who had been chronically depressed for years. Apparently, children who have to nurture their parents tend to view intimate relationships as oppressive. That's why they develop unrequited longings for people who never give them the time of day. Hence, my goal was to have a relationship with someone who was actually available. Perhaps I would grow to become attracted to

Connie . . . that is, if she was attracted to me. At our first dinner, I wasn't so sure.

But a few days later, the phone rang. It was Connie, asking me if I wanted to go out to dinner again. I thought, "Why not?" No one else was beating my door down, as they say.

"Sure," I said.

So we dated for a month or so. We were sitting in a coffee shop near Rittenhouse Square in Philly when Connie invited me down to San Antonio for a long weekend.

"I'll pay for your fare with my frequent flyer miles," she said. After I overcame my surprise, I agreed. The fact that I hadn't known her all that long didn't deter me. She seemed nice. She *was* nice. In some ways she was nicer than I was. She was much more outgoing, anyway . . . always talking about her co-workers and her friends at home with genuine warmth. I found this refreshing. Besides, I had never been to Texas. And I had heard that San Antonio was by far the prettiest city in the state.

Since there is no direct service between Philadelphia and San Antonio, I had to change planes in Houston. When I landed in San Antonio, Connie was standing near the exit, a big smile on her face. After driving me to her home, a two story, vaguely Spanish style tract house, we had dinner at a nearby restaurant. The next day, she showed me the sights. We strolled around San Antonio's famed River Walk, which was colorful and busy. We toured the site of the 1968 World's Fair and saw the Tower of the Americas. And of course we saw the Alamo. It was smaller than I had imagined it, but impressive nonetheless. Since there were now tall office buildings all around it, it was hard to associate with a bloody battle.

That evening, Connie introduced me to her friends. We sat around a fire pit at her neighbor Danny's house and drank wine. Danny was a government worker who was married to Laurie, a nurse. Their friend Mark worked in communications for the University of Texas, San Antonio. He also played bass for a jazz combo that performed at the River Walk. Mark was divorced. Danny and Mark were good guys. They were both that endangered species: Texas liberals. Neither had a problem with gays; however, Connie said that Laurie was a devout Catholic and did not really like her. Connie had known them all since high school. It said something about them that they had remained friends. Connie said she didn't have any gay friends in San Antonio. She missed having gay friends. Evidently the gay scene in San Antonio wasn't all that hot.

That Saturday, we drove to Lyndon Johnson's ranch in the Hill Country. On the way, I asked Connie about the phrase, "Don't Mess With Texas." I said it sounded belligerent.

"Oh," she laughed. "That was just a slogan from an anti-littering campaign."

I was a little relieved. You never knew about Texas, what with that disaster, George W. Bush.

When we got to the LBJ Ranch, We saw the tiny house where LBJ was born and the Pedernales River, which twisted like a corkscrew through the property.

"You call that a river?" I kidded Connie. I guess I was chauvinistic about the Delaware.

"Sometimes it floods," she replied. As our guided tour bus pulled closer to the Texas White House, we saw a group of people sitting out front on the porch. The bus driver mentioned that Lady Bird Johnson—who was now in her nineties—still came out here from time to time. Just then, from out of the crowd, a woman waved to us. Although we weren't close enough to get a really good look, for all we knew it could have been Lady Bird. For a lifelong liberal, this was about as good as it gets.

"I read that LBJ's mother was extremely religious and that his dad drank too much," I told Connie.

"That describes half the couples in Texas," she replied. I laughed.

That evening, Connie and I sat drinking beer on her couch and watched comedy videos on her hi-def TV. Connie was a big fan of certain stand-up comedians.

"Is Wanda Sykes gay?" I asked Connie.

"I don't know," Connie said. This was before Wanda had come out.

By the end of the weekend, I had come out. Although the plan was for Connie to sleep on the couch and me to sleep in her bed, we began getting intimate on the couch. It was probably the alcohol. Also, I hadn't had sex with anyone for ten years. Ten years!

I was kind of shocked at myself since I had made the first move. Afterward, I felt like throwing up.

"I kind of feel queasy," I told Connie.

Needless to say, she was disconcerted. She had probably never met anyone whom sleeping with had made physically ill. It wasn't her, per se. It was nerves. The whole thing had been too abrupt. Here I was 2000 miles from home, having sex with a woman I hardly knew. I hastened to assure Connie that I wanted to continue to see her.

So we did. Connie would come up to South Jersey on Sunday afternoons and leave for Texas on Thursday afternoons. Sometimes I'd spend the night with her at her room at the Holiday Inn.

"You live an anomic life," I told her. I told her that *anomie* meant disoriented and disconnected. But she didn't mind her life. It didn't seem to bother her to spend so much time in hotel rooms and airports and rental cars. In fact, she seemed rather proud of being able to commute such a long distance. She spent a lot of time listening to podcasts on her iPod. She was a big fan of NPR. Also, she said that if she continued earning good money as a defense consultant, she could retire in a few years.

As our relationship continued, I became much more comfortable around Connie. But it was clear that I was never going to become passionately attracted to her. I liked her, but she wanted more. She had every right to expect passion. So, for that matter, did I.

It was awkward. Still, we continued to see each other. That summer, we decided to take an Olivia Cruise of Alaska. For those of you who don't know, Olivia is a tour company for lesbians. The whole ship would be lesbians, except, of course, for the crew. Connie graciously offered to pay for half of my fare. Since she was making much bigger bucks than I was, how could I refuse?

There's nothing like breaking up on a cruise ship. It's not as if one can go anywhere. The ship sailed from Vancouver, Canada. The crunch came our first night out of harbor. We both got drunk, Connie more so than I.

That night, when we were in bed, Connie said, "This is awful." I had tried to reciprocate her passion, but it was clear to Connie that my heart just wasn't in it. By the way, anyone who thinks that lesbian sex is by nature hot is living in a dream world. It can be just as dull as hetero sex, if not duller. Ever heard of lesbian bed death? That occurred pretty quickly in my relationship with Connie.

Connie was by now very angry with me. I was messing up her romantic vacation. I should have told her earlier that I just wasn't all that into her physically. But I liked her company. I liked her warmth. I was afraid of being alone again.

Seeing all this beautiful scenery in the company of a person who doesn't want to be around you is a bittersweet experience—more bitter than sweet, actually. I knew that Connie resented me. She began giving me the cold shoulder. Still, she tried to make the most of the trip. We saw the totem pole village outside of Juneau. Connie developed a cold, so I did the tour of Skagway—the gold rush town—alone. There were lots of little shacks there, lining a lane. The woman who conducted the walking tour said that they had been used by prostitutes for quickies. Prostitution was a big thing in gold rush camps. We learned that the miners paid the whores in golden nuggets.

A day later, Connie and I went on a whale watching excursion together. We saw plenty of whales—blowing out water and breeching in spectacular fashion. We also saw some eagles, swooping above the deep blue water and alighting on the pine trees that lined the shore. I was torn between feeling awe for the breathtaking scenery and the whales and embarrassment at being in the company of someone who thought I was a jerk.

The next day, we took a bird-watching hike in Sitka. Since it was raining, we didn't see many birds—just a few kingfishers. But we did see a lot of salmon that had been half-eaten by bears. Evidently bears are sloppy eaters. Then we took the train ride to Anchorage and endured the long flight back to Houston and then Philly. Connie had her iPod in her ear, so she didn't have to talk to me very much. I tried to keep busy reading Zora Neale Hurston's *Their Eyes Were Watching God*. After getting the rental car at the Philly airport, Connie dumped me at my house like a sack of potatoes. Then she headed off to the Holiday Inn. She had to be at work the next day. I knew I had deeply disappointed her. She certainly deserved more than my lukewarm ass.

It's hard to disappoint a nice person. I knew that my therapist meant well in advising me to become involved with someone who was emotionally available. But one can't fake desire. On the basis of my awful Alaskan vacation, I resolved never to become involved with someone to whom I wasn't passionately attracted. But I broke that resolution fairly quickly when I met another Texan named Dawn.

As for Connie, she and I stayed in touch long enough for her to tell me she went on another Olivia cruise and thoroughly enjoyed herself. This time she went alone.

Ten White Russians

I was standing near the dance floor at Sisters Nightclub with my friend Donna, gazing at women who were presumably having a good time. Although Donna was straight, she sometimes accompanied me to the club. She was my closest friend.

"I like dancing where men won't hit on you," Donna liked to say. That was her rationale for accompanying me to lesbian bars. Except for sexuality, we had a lot in common. We were both feminists, for one thing. Donna, in particular, couldn't stand aggressive men. She had once had a bad experience with an aggressive man. In fact, she told me that she had been raped while she was living in Los Angeles.

"It was a guy who was a friend of my roommate. He pulled a gun on me one day when no one else was around," she said.

"That must have been awful!" I cried. "Did you press charges?"

"No," Donna said. "I probably should have, but I just couldn't go through all that."

It must have been traumatizing, but at the moment Donna told me, she didn't seem particularly broken up by it. Then again, she wasn't the type to go on and on about her emotions. Well, she was now in therapy, so maybe that was helping.

We watched the throng of women gyrate on Sisters' dance floor. It was chill and dark and, from my point of view, perpetually disappointing. With the pulsating dance music, it was like a cold, smoky womb. I almost never met women in clubs. I was shy and intellectual—not a good combination in the club world.

I noticed that Donna was really knocking them down. Her drink was White Russians. Since we had arrived, she had had several of the sweet, milky drinks. We had sat for a while at the downstairs bar before heading upstairs.

"Let's dance!" Donna had cried after about half an hour of that. You had to hand it to her—she had plenty of energy. Sometimes I thought she liked Sisters more than I did. After we walked upstairs, she placed her large pocketbook in one corner of the dance floor, and we swayed to the sound of "Like a Prayer." It was like we were two planets in different orbits. It wasn't erotic at all, but it was better than staying at home, for both of us.

Donna had broken up with her boyfriend Joe about a year earlier. That had been a mess. I had visited them on election night 1992, thinking that after twelve years of Republican rule it would be fun to celebrate Bill Clinton's election with friends. However, when I walked in the door of their apartment, the tension between the two hit me like a wave. At this point in their relationship, Donna kept watching and hectoring Joe. She got this way at times. Any little innocuous thing you said, she would jump on, like a vulture on road kill.

"It's a nice day today," you could say, and she'd read something into it.

"What did you say?" she'd ask, her green eyes lit with an unearthly gleam. "What do you mean by that?"

I'd try to explain that I meant nothing by it, but even that was difficult to do. She'd question your statement that you meant nothing, so you couldn't win.

That night we watched the election returns roll in. As we sat waiting for Clinton to address the crowd, Donna remembered that she was out of cereal and sent Joe to the Acme to get some. Then, when he was there, she called the store to page him to tell him to get something else. This was before cell phones became commonplace. That's something I would never do to anyone—have him or her paged over a supermarket loudspeaker. Whatever the hell she wanted him to pick up—mustard, celery, crackers—could wait.

"Donna could aggravate Jesus Christ off the Cross," Donna's mom had once told me. I had to reluctantly agree this was true. Yet I appreciated Donna's wit. She told me

that her mom had dropped out of Villanova after her dad graduated so that she could marry him and set up house.

"All Mom got from Villanova was her MRS. degree," Donna cracked.

When Joe came home from the Acme, he looked grim and put-upon.

"Did you get the mustard?" Donna asked him.

"Yes," he said as he placed the bag of groceries on the kitchen table.

"Did you get the Special K?"

"I told you I would," said Joe.

Tiring of the tense atmosphere, I made up some excuse and left a few minutes later. I never did see Bill Clinton address the crowd in Little Rock.

"Damn," I thought as I was walking to my car, "a Democrat finally gets elected president, and I spend the evening in the company of those two." I felt cheated. Who knew how long it would be before we once again had cause to celebrate?

Soon afterward, Donna began calling me and complaining that people were breaking into their apartment and moving things around.

A little while later, my jeweler friend Karen, who was Joe's coworker at Crosby Jewelers, and the woman who had introduced me to Donna, told me that Joe was ready to move out of the apartment.

"Donna was threatening him," Karen told me over the phone.

"What?!"

"Yes, threatening." Karen sighed. "I feel guilty that I introduced them."

At this point you might wonder why I had Donna as a friend. Her behavior was obviously crazy. As I later learned, believing that people are entering your home when you're not there is a common delusion among schizophrenics. Yet, the truth is that Donna could be a wonderful companion. At her best she was effervescent. We had a great time watching movies together. It seems a simple thing to have a friend to do that with, but if you're gay it's not that easy.

For one thing, I've never lived in a community where gay women are abundant. Frankly, there aren't many places like that in the world. Secondly, I found that many straight women were either freaked out by lesbians or else they tried to seduce them. They weren't really interested in a relationship; they just wanted to see if they could. Donna wasn't freaked out by me, nor did she try to seduce me. She appreciated gay people, in part because her older brother Jimmy had been gay.

"My parents found a love letter that a guy had written to Jimmy," Donna told me soon after we had first met, at a Buddhist meeting. "My dad was furious!" Furious, over someone's sexuality! Well, her parents had met at a Catholic university.

Donna adored Jimmy. She told me how handsome he was.

"Jimmy lived for a while in New York and met Arthur Laurents," Donna told me.

"Who's Arthur Laurents?" I asked.

"He wrote the book for West Side Story*."*

I envisioned Jimmy leading the high life in Manhattan, a gorgeous young gay man amidst the artistic elite.

But Donna never could catch a break: beloved Jimmy died of AIDS in the early nineties. Donna didn't talk much about him after that, and I never saw her distraught. However, his death must have been heart-wrenching for her.

After we stopped dancing, she went to the ladies' room. When she came out, she went over to the bar and ordered another White Russian. I was just finishing off my first beer. I marveled at her capacity. She started chatting with a couple of flannel-clad women who were standing near us. She was far more outgoing than I. As Donna chatted with the two women, I became emboldened and walked up to a woman who had been standing by the dance floor.

"Want to dance?" I shouted over the music.

The woman, a stocky brunette with short hair, nodded, and we danced to "Love Shack."

But I noticed her eyes shifting around the dance floor. When the song ended, we thanked each other and went our separate ways.

Donna went to the bar and returned with another White Russian.

We danced a bit more and then Donna had another drink.

I danced with another woman. The night wore on. Time slides by in dance clubs. The beat becomes hypnotic.

"How many drinks have you had, Donna?" I asked her.

"Ten," she said, smiling. By now her eyes were gleaming like neon signs.

"Ten!" I would have been on the floor after three. But Donna was strange that way. She seemed immune to the effects of alcohol consumption. It was as if her stomach was disconnected from her brain.

Well, it didn't matter that much. I was driving, and I had had two lite beers.

I worried about Donna, though. Sometimes her lips moved and no words came out.

"I used to hear voices," she once told me, quite casually, as we were driving down Route 70 in Plum Hill. She could have been describing any other mundane thing that people do, such as shopping at a particular store or having a certain job. *I used to hear voices.*

"Do you still hear them?" I asked her.

"No," she said. But I think she still did. I suspected she was talking to the voices in her head, having a regular back and forth with them. I was appalled. This was some heavy-duty shit.

"Are you still chanting?" I asked her. As a Nichiren Buddhist, I chant for roughly an hour a day. It centers me. I thought that chanting might lessen any voices that Donna might be hearing.

"No," she said. "That only makes me worse."

I didn't know what to say. I wanted to help Donna, but there didn't seem to be a way. She was already seeing a therapist, and she refused to admit that she was now hearing voices. I wondered if she was on medication, but I was afraid to ask her.

Sometimes I berated myself for having a best friend who was obviously crazy. What did that say about me? That I felt most at home around nutty people? But Donna wasn't *just* crazy. Sometimes she said wise things. One evening I was ragging about my older brother Steve and the fact that he was still smoking. Donna sighed and said, "You did your best to get him to quit. You just have to accept people for what they are." She also told me that I was wasting my time mooning over some woman I worked with.

"Ruth, you're like that Leslie Howard character in *Of Human Bondage!*" she once told me. "He had a club foot, and he was nuts over some trampy woman who was way beneath him."

Although it hurt to hear this, I had to acknowledge that Donna was dead right about my infatuation with my co-worker Jeannie. I had to face the fact that Jeannie just wasn't that into me. She never had been and never would be.

About three years after the trip to Sisters, Donna's husband Nick called me on the phone. He and Donna had been married only a couple of years. They had met at the office where they both worked. Donna had introduced me to Nick, and I had thought he was a nice, cute guy. The thought had occurred to me to warn him about Donna, but there was no way I could have done that. Besides, her symptoms were in abeyance, and she seemed so happy.

"What's up?" I asked him now. I was surprised he was calling me. He never called me; Donna did.

"What's up?" repeated Nick, as if subtly mocking my casual tone. "Donna is dead," he said.

I felt the ground sway beneath me. I sat down on my bed, which was next to the phone.

"I got home from work and found her dead on the bathroom floor," Nick continued. He went on to tell me that Donna had been bulimic and had also been diagnosed as schizophrenic.

"I never realized she was bulimic!"

"Well, I couldn't miss it, living with her," Nick replied. He told me that she had been going to the county mental health clinic for treatment, but they hadn't done much for her.

I wasn't surprised by their lack of success. It wasn't like she had been going to a high priced private therapist. Yet I chided myself for missing the bulimia. We were best friends. What clues had I missed?

I thought back to the night of the ten White Russians. Had Donna been puking them up in the bathroom? She didn't look particularly thin. Then again, as I later learned, many bulimics are normal weight. Also, it was hard to gauge just how much she weighed because she often wore baggy sweaters. Since she and Nick had moved up to Jenkintown, I hadn't seen her as much as I had when she was living in Collingswood. In fact, I hadn't seen her in two months. She used to call me up a lot, though. In fact, in the month or so before she died, she would call me constantly, every evening.

"Hi Ruth," she'd say.

"Hi Donna," I'd reply. "What's happening?"

"Nothing much," she'd say. Then she'd say, "Well, I just wanted to say hello. That's all. Good-bye."

Then she'd call again fifteen minutes later and do the same thing. When I asked her why she kept calling me and to please stop, she wouldn't give a reason, but would promise not to call me anymore. But then fifteen minutes later she'd do it again.

I started not answering the phone.

"Fuck!" I'd cry when the phone rang. I felt like tearing my hair out.

I called Karen and told her what was happening.

"Call the police on her," Karen said. She said that, but I don't think that's what she would have done. Karen is a very compassionate Buddhist. I couldn't call the police on Donna either, no matter that she was getting on my last nerve. She was my closest friend.

"The coroner said she weighed   seventy-five pounds," said Nick. "He's doing a blood test, but he thinks that her heart might have just stopped. That can happen with eating disorders."

I pictured Donna lying dead on the cold bathroom tiles. Maybe she had been vomiting when her heart stopped. It was all such a come down. I knew that she had had high expectations for her marriage and had truly loved Nick. I speculated that when even being happily married didn't cure her demons, she went on a downhill slide.

"Poor Donna," I thought. I went to my Gohonzon and chanted for her.

A few days later, Nick called to tell me that the blood test hadn't revealed anything.

"Someone from the mental health clinic called to find out if Donna was going to keep her next appointment," he added. I can only imagine how he felt upon being asked that.

I had one question for Nick. "Did you know that Donna had mental problems before you married her?"

"Yes," Nick said. But he married her anyway. That was Donna.

Shortly after she died, I entered therapy. I felt that this was one "life event" I couldn't handle on my own. When I told my therapist about Donna's death, she said, in effect, that Donna had too many serious problems, and it was best that she had been released from this vale of tears.

"We enter this world crying, while everyone around us is happy," said my therapist. "We leave this world happy to be at peace, while everyone around us is crying."

What she said made sense. This life is no picnic for anyone. And as I looked back on Donna's life, I realized that she had never, *ever* been at peace. Perhaps now she was.

Three or four months before she died, Donna brought me a Chunky candy bar. I have no idea why. I hadn't asked for it. She just breezed into my apartment one evening and said that she had bought one for herself and that she wanted me to have one, too. I wasn't hungry, so I put the Chunky in my refrigerator and forgot about it.

It was still sitting there, behind the milk, when Nick called to tell me of Donna's death.

Thirteen years later, I still have the Chunky. I can't bring myself to throw it out. It's like a silver ingot brought up from a mine. Now that I look back on it, I think that Donna might have given it to me as a clue to her eating disorder. She couldn't tell me directly that she was bulimic; she just hinted at it—with food.

Sometimes I think that if I ever get money, I will donate a lot of it to research into eating disorders and schizophrenia. That would be a worthwhile thing to do.

It's been thirteen years since Donna died. In that time, I've made new friends and had lovers. Yet Donna remains the closest friend I've ever had. She was a charming amalgam of kindness, light-heartedness, loyalty, insight, and heavy-duty mental illness.

I remember her at her best.

IMMACULATE

I was sitting in a chair at the foot of my mother's death bed, writing a piece about the "Immaculate Reception" for a book of true-life sports stories for teens. For those of you who are unfamiliar with football, the "Immaculate Reception" refers to an incredible play made in a playoff game between the Pittsburgh Steelers and the Oakland Raiders back in 1973. It happened like this: with just seconds left to play, Pittsburgh quarterback Terry Bradshaw threw a desperation pass. Instead of his receiver Frenchy Fuqua catching the ball, it seemed to carom off the shoulder pad of Oakland defender Jack Tatum and back toward the Steelers, where Steelers running back Franco Harris adroitly caught it before it touched the ground and sprinted into the end zone for the game-winning touchdown. There was considerable controversy about this play. If the ball had touched Fuqua and not Tatum, Harris's catch would have been ruled illegal. But the officials ruled that the ball had touched Tatum and not Fuqua and thus, Harris's reception could stand. In other words, it was an "immaculate reception."

I enjoyed researching this story. However, it *was* a bit odd writing about it in the same room where my mother lay dying. I should explain that there was nothing anyone could do for my mother at this point. She was quite old and was no longer able to swallow food without it getting into her lungs. Aspiration of food causes infection and, inevitably, death. My mother had been in a coma for several days now. Although we couldn't be sure that she was insensate, she was certainly unresponsive. All the nursing home staff could do was to turn her every so often so that she wouldn't get bedsores, give her morphine, and swab out her mouth with water.

As I looked up from my laptop, I studied my mother's face. Her eyes were closed. She was wrinkled and shriveled.

In a sense, the hard part was over, the part where she knew what was happening. During her last stay in the hospital, a week earlier, she had thanked me for taking care of her. She knew I loved her. Her death was just a matter of time. Her sepulchral immobility stood (lay?) in stark contrast to the action-filled world I was writing about. All her actions in this life, except for the rise and fall of her chest, were at an end.

A nurse came into the room. She looked at my mother.

"She's taking a while," she commented, not unkindly. "Sometimes it helps if you tell them they can go."

A few minutes later, I got a call on my cell phone from my sister Janet and brother-in-law Carl in Arkansas. I told them what was happening and what the nurse had said. I put the phone to my mother's ear. I didn't catch what my sister said, but I heard Carl tell my mother, "You gave me Janet, and I thank you for that." I hope my mother, in the depths of her coma, heard that.

After the call, I held my mother's hand for a while. Then I went back to my laptop. My mother would have approved. Although she had never said as much, I could tell that she had been frustrated over never having had a career. Being a stay-at-home mother hadn't been enough for her, but she lacked the confidence to do anything else. Don't believe the bullshit that some people tell you. If you have more intelligence than a carrot, being a stay-at-home mother all your life isn't enough. Thus, my becoming a professional writer pleased my mother: in a small way, I helped assuage her thwarted ambition.

So I continued to type. I had especially enjoyed reading about Steelers quarterback Terry Bradshaw. People had underestimated him at the beginning of his career, called him a hick and a jerk. But he showed them by winning four Super Bowl rings.

Yes, my mother would heartily approve of my writing in the room where she died.

Acknowledgements

"Pagan Heaven" was published in volume 20 of *American Writing* in 2000.

"On Mickle Street," "Mona," "Visionary," and "Narcotic" were published in *Woman 2 Woman*, January/February, 2004.

"Narcotic" was published in *White Crow*, volume 6, issue 2, 2004.

"Resting Places," "Renaissance" "Spoken Word" and "Ode to a Parking Garage" were published in *Philadelphia Poets* in April 2005, October 2005, April 2006, April 2007, and April 2010 respectively. "Benediction," "The Bronze God," and "Schuylkill" were published in *Philadelphia Poets*, April 2013, April 2014 and April 2015, respectively.

"The Thirteenth Sign" and "Grand Tour" were published in *Rio: An Online Journal* of SUNY at Stonybrook in 2005.

"Close" was published in the *Coal City Review*.

"Mona" was published in *Mona Poetica*, an anthology of poetry about the Mona Lisa, published by Mayapple Press in 2005.

"Madonna della Cucina" was published in the 2009 edition of *Mad Poets Review*.

"Replacing Phil" was published in *Sangam*, an online literary magazine.

"Hermitage" was published in *SNReview.org* in Winter/Spring 2012

"Immaculate" was published in *Four Ties Lit Review* in Issue 1, Volume 2, 2011.

"Romance: was published in *SnReview.org* in Fall/Winter, 2013

"Let Mike Do It" appeared in the anthology *This Assignment is So Gay,* published by Sibling Rivalry Press in 2013.

"Zip" was published by *Wilde Magazine* in Fall, 2013.

"The Phillies, Dick Allen, and Me" was published in *winningwriters.com* in Fall, 2014.

"Spook Show" was published in *Bullmensfiction.com* in November, 2015.

"Aquaria" was published in *Philadelphia Stories*, Summer, 2016

"Mess With Texas" was published in the anthology, *Dispatches from Lesbian America*, published by Bedazzled Ink, 2016.

Ruth Rouff is an English instructor and freelance writer living in Collingswood, New Jersey. After earning a BA in English from Vassar College and a MS in Education from Saint Joseph's University, she has taught for a number of years in Philadelphia and Camden NJ. Her work has appeared in various literary journals, including *Exquisite Corpse*, *Philadelphia Poets*, and *Wilde*. In addition, she has written two young adult nonfiction books: *Ida B. Wells: A Woman of Courage* and *Great Moments in Sports*.